Where the Cobbled Path Leads

ADVANCE PRAISE FOR THE AUTHOR

Where
~ the ~
Cobbled
Path Leads

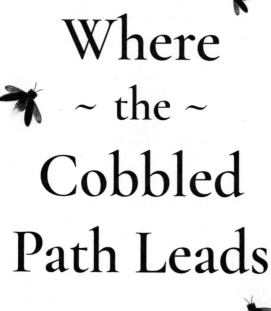

AVINUO KIRE

PENGUIN

An imprint of Penguin Random House

HAMISH HAMILTON

USA | Canada | UK | Ireland | Australia
New Zealand | India | South Africa | China

Hamish Hamilton is part of the Penguin Random House group of companies
whose addresses can be found at global.penguinrandomhouse.com

Published by Penguin Random House India Pvt. Ltd
4th Floor, Capital Tower 1, MG Road,
Gurugram 122 002, Haryana, India

Penguin
Random House
India

First published in Hamish Hamilton by Penguin Random House India 2022

10 9 8 7 6 5 4 3

ISBN 9780670096794

Typeset in Bembo Std by Manipal Technologies Limited, Manipal
Printed at Thomson Press India Ltd, New Delhi

www.penguin.co.in

MIX
Paper
FSC FSC® C010615

For Javor
A Keneithoyo

CONTENTS

ONE

In these sleepy little hill towns, there is a secret path every child knows, a trail every nostalgic adult remembers. Sometimes, they lead to river holes and secret hideouts, other times, to a beloved; perhaps a grandparent or best friend. Vime's special place was the very path itself—a crumbling cobbled mossed walkway, level ground playfully interlacing with stairs, minuscule wild daisies and cudweed on the grooves and edges, winding in, out, trailing further and further down into the deepest woods. The narrow lane effortlessly navigated between rows of cottages on one side and the forest against mist-cloaked hills and perennial evergreen trees on the other. It had been built by local coolies hired by the British many decades ago. Vime didn't know where the footpath ended. She had never been so far.

Mrs Sebu threw open her window just as Vime was passing by. 'Neinuo', the woman called out affectionately, using the local term of endearment meaning 'little one'.

'Where might you be off to this fine afternoon?'

'Oh, hello Aunty . . . umm . . . nowhere in particular',
feeling self-conscious, Vime muttered her words, politely
slowing her pace but not stopping either. Mrs Sebu was one
of the kindest adults Vime knew, but she was in no mood
to talk to anyone this morning. Not even Aunty Sebu who
occasionally invited her in for tea, particularly when she had
just baked her famed Kemenya cake. She felt the woman's
curious gaze upon her back even as she resumed her pace.

Poor thing, Mrs Sebu clicked her tongue in sympathy
as her gaze lingered upon Vime's willowy retreating figure.
She mentally calculated how long it had been since Vime's
mother had passed. Asshh kijü kelhou ha, a young girl
like Vime needs a mother, Mrs Sebu reflected with a sad
heavy sigh.

Today was, in fact, Mother's first death anniversary.
Father's eyes were suspiciously bloodshot in the morning
but no one commented, not Vime nor Neime, her elder
sister. Last evening, they had together laid white calla lilies,
freshly picked from the fields, upon Mother's grave. They
were Mother's favourite flowers and when she was alive,
seeing the tall-stemmed white flowers lean heavy against
Mother's earth-soiled khorü basket was evidence that she
had just returned from the field. Someone would then
randomly call out, 'Mother, Apfo, where are you?'. Not
for any particular reason but because that's what you do
in homes with a mother. Last evening, however, despite
the once-comforting presence of white calla lilies, no one
spoke a word—not even to each other. Forlorn thoughts
pined and weighed heavy in the air as the sepia-tinted
evening sun gently went down behind them. Mother
would have said a prayer, she'd have known the right

words to say, Vime had thought, her insides cold; numb and clammy.

Vime's own memories of Mother were iridescent—alive with luminous sun-drenched colours, pulsating with faint echoes of laughter. Mother had been a joyful soul, always filled with irrepressible mirth that seemed ready to burst into peals of laughter with the slightest provocation. Her laughter was so infectious that Vime often imagined it travelled for miles around. Sometimes in the marketplace, complete strangers would find themselves unconsciously grinning over the rollicking sound of Mother's hearty and somewhat masculine laughter. Teenaged Neime would sometimes feel embarrassed over Mother's uninhibited gaiety in public but not Vime, not ever. She admired her mother's spirit, her unabashed hearty appetite for life.

It seemed that their vivacious mother's effervescent presence had sustained life in their home all along. With her gone, their centre was now lost. Their once bustling house was now haunted with a devouring silence which left nothingness in its trace; a stunned open-mouthed gaping with no sound for relief. These days, sad little sighs sometimes escaped lonely concrete nooks and corners. The melancholy was contagious. Even the house plants looked drab and sickly, although Neime and Vime faithfully watered the plants in turn, as taught by Mother. After getting sick and learning that she did not have long to live, Mother had left her all-too-young daughters a list of detailed instructions on how to maintain the house after she was gone. But of course, no amount of training can fill the void a mother leaves. Vime understood well that the house, too, was in mourning, along with its occupants.

This afternoon, after changing out of her school uniform, Vime darted out the house, towards the cobbled footpath at the end of the road. This had been her favourite escape when Mother was alive and she was glad it had remained unchanged.

Not ready to return home, Vime listlessly skipped down the path, past the old kharü, village gate, with fierce animals and warriors holding human heads etched onto its ancient wood. As the village rapidly expanded and developed into a township, the landscape changed and the dilapidated village gate no longer served its purpose. However, because of the fearful taboos associated with destroying a sacred kharü, the locals had left the gate untouched while constructing the lane.

Vime continued her solitary walk until there were no longer any houses in sight; only a lone footpath accompanied by miles of inviting sun-kissed paddy fields with the sheaves bound, ripe and ready for harvest. Finally, the meandering footpath tapered towards a rather majestic looking tree with vines tumbling and wizened branches embracing the skies, creating a resplendent canopy of forest up high. The tree's sturdy gnarled roots generously sprawled over the ground, extending deep into the earth, all the way down to a little babbling brook below. As a fascinated Vime curiously drew closer to inspect the tree, she tripped upon a stray tree root. The next thing she knew, she had fallen down, quite comfortably to her surprise, neatly propped and cushioned within a nest of vines at the foot of the tree. Her feet ached and the balmy weather made her feel deliciously drowsy all of a sudden. She decided to stay and rest awhile.

Vime was awakened by the mournful chorus of the cicadas. A deep cerulean dusk was setting in quickly.

She had involuntarily fallen into deep sleep. Alarm crept as she realized that it would surely be dark before she could reach home. Scrambling up her feet, Vime hastily brushed dirt and grass off her clothes and prepared to head home. But to her bewildered dismay, she saw that there was no footpath where she knew it ought to be. Unease gathered as she strained her eyes but she could still see nothing except the lush forest floor surrounded by distant lonely fields and the stream below. Vime slowly walked around the massive tree, completely mystified. She tried to retrace her steps but there was nothing familiar to retrace, save the cozy little spot she had fallen and slept upon.

Autumn dusk was rapidly giving way to darkness now and Vime felt tears welling. This day had begun miserably and was ending even worse, she thought. As she allowed herself to give in to helpless tears and sniffles, she heard a shuffling sound. She turned round to discover a girl her age, coolly looking at her as if she had been there the entire time. Startled, Vime stared dumbly.

The girl spoke first. 'Shuush there! What's wrong? You're going to wake everyone up with your snivelling.'

The petite girl had her hands on her hips in a patronizing manner but her tone sounded more earnest than unkind. She was nice looking enough but oddly attired. She wore a black top and neikhronei, the kind that very young girls were traditionally supposed to wear. Vime had never seen anyone her age, wear such clothing except in rare old photographs or during culturally-themed programmes at school. Feeling embarrassed to be caught crying like a child, Vime wiped her eyes and quickly composed herself.

'I'm sorry. I've had a bad day.'

'It's alright.'

'Could you please direct me to the footpath that leads to the main road? I don't know how, but I seem to have lost my way.'

Vime thought she saw a mischievous glint in the girl's quick watchful eyes but it was hastily replaced with warm sympathy.

'Oh, you're lost? Don't cry, it's right here, behind this tree', saying this, the girl promptly took her hand. Vime allowed the girl to guide her around the tree's massive trunk, all the while feebly protesting that she had already looked there.

'No, it's not there, I've already searched . . . ', Vime began, but to her embarrassed disconcertment, the familiar footpath was right behind the tree all along. Relief washed over her and she grinned sheepishly. I must really be exhausted, Vime decided. She thanked the girl and asked,

'Do you live nearby? How are you here so late?'

'Oh, I live here', the girl replied with nonchalant alacrity.

Vime had so many questions, but she was anxious to get home so she thanked the strange girl again and started to leave. Just then, the girl spoke:

'I know a secret place where the sweetest juiciest wild raspberries are always in season. Would you like me to take you there?' She looked incredibly lonesome suddenly and Vime felt sorry for her. She knew what loneliness felt like.

But she replied instead: 'I'd love to but another day perhaps? It's kind of a special day today and my family will be waiting for me', Vime explained. It suddenly struck her then that she had not thought of Mother for the longest time. Today of all days! she marvelled inwardly.

'I understand. Please come again soon. I'll be here. I'm always here', the girl replied and disappeared around the back of the tree before Vime had a chance to say goodbye.

'I will. Well, see you then', Vime called out to the empty darkness anyway.

TWO

It was some time before Vime could wander down the cobbled trail again. Her grandparents had been visiting when she reached home that fateful night. Grandmother had been wracked with anxiety and had promptly burst into relieved tears the moment Vime stepped foot inside the house.

'Atsa, I'm alright, I'm fine. I just went for a walk', Vime mumbled as her grandmother fussed and engulfed her in a tight embrace while Grandfather patted both their backs and comforted Grandmother.

'There now dear, Vime is home, she's fine like she said.'

Father had gone out to search for her and Neime had to go get him. Instead of scolding her as she had feared, father had looked immensely guilty, like it was his fault that Vime had gone 'missing' as they all insisted, no matter how many times Vime repeated that she had simply gone for a walk and lost track of time. She decided not to tell them about the strange girl and how she had gotten lost. It would only upset them further.

Vime thought that Neime had been uncharacteristically understanding over the entire episode that night. Rather than Father, she had been bracing herself for a condescending lecture from her older sister and had been subconsciously prepared to go on the defensive. But criticism of her tardiness never came. And so, in wordless gratitude, Vime had been making a conscious effort to stay home and help more around the house since.

It was not easy, she thought.

'Vimenuo, how many times do I have to tell you to turn the laundry inside out and clip them properly? What if the wind blows them away?', Neime grumbled as she proceeded to clip the fresh laundry which Vime had just done, dripping wet and spread over the entire length of the clothesline. Vime felt a sharp twinge of irritation over how Neime in reprimanding her, used her full name just like Mother used to do.

'And squeeze the water out properly before you hang them', Neime continued peevishly while Vime childishly stuck her tongue out and continued reading her storybook with an exaggerated show of nonchalance.

She heard her sister storm off angrily and felt a tad guilty afterwards. In the past, Neime would have run off to Mother to complain about her bad behaviour. Mother would then reproof Vime for her unladylike conduct while Neime looked on in smug satisfaction, an expression Vime found quite intolerably, quintessentially Neime. She'd say something cutting which would invariably set Neime off and their quarrel would begin all over again. It was odd how Neime never thought of complaining to Father. He was always around and yet he was not. One would have imagined that Father was utterly unaffected by their constant bickering. But then there was that one time when they had been hotly arguing, each trying to outshout the other, when Father suddenly intervened by firmly grabbing each by the arm. He proceeded to drag the two sisters inside the dark little storeroom kept for storing grain and said:

'Enough! I've had enough of your constant squabbling. There, now go ahead and kill each other. See if I care!' Saying this, Father had locked the two of them inside the room, stunned and rendered silent by their normally reticent father's outburst.

Vime grimly wondered why Neime and she brought out the worst in each other. She thought her sister was perfectly nice and amenable towards everyone but her. Everyone seemed to admire Neime because she was always demure and perfectly gracious in public while she, Vime, was socially awkward and never knew the right things to say, not like Neime. Vime truly believed that except for Mother, anyone else would choose Neime over her.

'You're the elder sister so you have to be more patient', Mother had often touted.

'But I'll always be older', Neime would promptly burst into indignant tears and righteous outrage. Neime cried easily but Vime noted that her sister's easy inclination to burst into tears had all but ceased in the recent past. On the contrary, much to Vime's chagrin, ever since Mother's demise, Neime had somehow taken it upon herself to become the mistress of the house, always fussing over housework and chiding Vime to clean up her room, just like Mother used to do. Although it annoyed her, Vime rarely talked back like she would have during life with

Mother. Vime didn't care to squabble with her sister like she used to, and aside from the occasional criticism, neither did Neime. One could say the fight had gone out of both girls now that Mother was not around to mend their little hurts and aches.

'Neime, I'm going out for a bit', Vime called out, carefully choosing her words so that it did not appear like she was asking for permission. Give Neime an inch, she'd take a mile, Vime thought, feeling very clever.

'Alright. But don't be too late. Where do you go exactly?' Neime asked, her eyes narrowing in suspicion. 'I met Khriebu the other day and she said she hasn't seen you for sometime now'.

'Just walking around', Vime shrugged evasively.

'Why don't you visit Khriebu?' Neime suggested, 'It's not right that she should be the one visiting you all the time.'

Avoiding her sister's gaze, Vime looked down and shifted her weight to the other foot, feeling uncomfortably guilty. Khriebu, who lived in the same neighborhood, had been her closest friend ever since she could remember. Their mothers had been wonderful friends, too. In the past, their mothers often did chores together while their young daughters played alongside. Khriebu and her mother, Apfo Neilaü, had been a great source of support the past year. But now Vime found it painful to see Khriebu. She knew she was being unfair but Khriebu reminded her of the irrevocability of what she had lost. Vime was painfully aware that she had been sullen and morose the last time Khriebu had visited and had actually felt relieved when her friend finally departed. Khriebu had not said anything but her clear brown eyes held perplexed hurt. They had not met since.

'Listen Vime.. .', Neime continued, 'It's not good to cut yourself off from people. You're either in your room and when you're not, you're always out wandering alone . . .'

'That's not true', Vime quickly interjected, warmth creeping up her ears and cheeks, feeling that it was most unfair of Neime to accuse her of staying out all the time. 'I haven't gone out since . . .', she couldn't bring herself to mention Mother's death anniversary, '. . . not since Atsa and Apfusta's visit', Vime finished weakly.

'Alright alright', Neime relented, taking on the kind of tone that one would use to placate a difficult child. 'Why don't you visit Khriebu instead of wandering alone by yourself? I'm sure she'll be happy to see you.'

Resisting the old urge to tell Neime it was none of her business, Vime muttered 'I'll try', instead, and made a hasty exit before Neime could respond.

THREE

Although Vime had given her word to visit her friend, albeit grudgingly, she found her feet irrevocably drawn towards the wayside. Vime had been unenthusiastically toying with the idea of visiting Khriebu but when she reached the crossroads, she had a strong sense that the sun favoured the other road, partially shining all its warm radiance towards the road leading to her favourite cobbled walkway. As Vime continued to linger at the intersection, feeling quite mystified, she heard strains of a melody from the nearby woodland. Although the forest song was muffled, it evocatively conjured blissful visions of children laughing in the woods amidst the happy gurgling of streams of water. The melody felt incredibly familiar to Vime and she felt almost certain that it was a song she had known once. A rush of bittersweet nostalgia overwhelmed her. She felt her feet undeniably drawn towards the forest song and so, she gladly gave in.

The forest song continued to maintain the same intensity regardless of the distance she covered but faded the moment she reached the cobbled walkway, which broke away from the main road. Vime felt her heart lurch with strange excitement. It had been so long since she had been moved by anything. Although the forest song had gone silent, she could still feel the notes reverberating inside her heart. Vime felt the wind behind nudge her forward. With heady abandonment, she dashed down the trail, consciously making a mental note of the time, aware that she shouldn't be late returning home this time round. She felt a heady rush of exhilaration and her feet felt ridiculously, effortlessly lightweight. It felt like the wind was literally spiriting her into the forest.

Within no time at all, Vime was once again beside the tree where she had met that strange girl. The forest was eerily quiet this afternoon, as if aware of the presence of an unknown visitor. No bird squawked overhead, she heard no chirping of birds or cries of insects; if fact, there was no indication of any animal life. Was it this quiet the last time? Vime wondered. She began exploring by walking around the tree, her fingers lightly brushing against its weathered bark. Wanting to meet the odd-looking girl again, Vime stood on tiptoes and strained her neck, looking around her surroundings, trying to spot nearby human habitats. But all she could see were Autumn trees and the little brook down below. If anything, the forest appeared denser than the last time she was here. Even the paddy fields she had passed appeared further away, looking like distant hazy yellow splotches. Minutes built but there was still no sign of life, let alone a girl. Vime inwardly berated herself for not having the presence of mind to ask the girl precisely where she lived. Never mind, she thought, she was determined not to let anything spoil the magical day.

'Hello there!' Vime called out playfully and the forest promptly answered with echoes.

'My name is Vime! What's yours?' Vime shouted unselfconsciously, with abandon.

Giggling over her own silliness, Vime sat herself down the same spot where she had fallen asleep the last time. The hairs on the back of her arms prickled as she instinctively sensed curious pairs of eyes on her. Intriguingly though, it was not an unpleasant sensation altogether. For some reason, being here all by her lonesome and yet feeling not entirely so, eased her loneliness. Sitting cross-legged, she looked up the tree with its great sturdy branches spiralling in all directions, up and around, blossoming to form an extraordinary dome of green, yellow and emerald foliage. Somewhere, a lone bird squawked, breaking the silence. Next thing, the skies darkened and Vime heard the gradual soft patter of light rain.

Unbothered, she stretched out her hands. 'I bet not a single drop of rain can get through you', she exclaimed confidently, looking up the seemingly impenetrable leafy ceiling. There was a deliberate rustle of leaves and as if in answer, a few leaves showered down her upturned face.

Vime was captivated. It truly felt like she was not alone. 'Where am I?' she stood up and asked in amazed wonder.

This time the tree was silent. Instead, a voice answered.

'You're late. You said you'd be back soon.' The speaker's voice sounded piqued.

Vime recognized the voice instantly without having to turn towards its direction. It was the same strange girl she had met that evening. Except that today, the girl looked different somehow. Vime couldn't be certain of this person's gender. The figure appeared naked except that he or she wasn't because there was no indication of any form of genitalia. Conscious that she was rudely staring, Vime feigned nonchalance and inquired:

'Oh, hello! Are you the same . . . girl I met that night?' Vime cautiously hesitated before uttering the word 'girl'. She didn't want to risk offending by assuming anything.

'Yes of course! Who else would I be?'

'Oh. You look different today', Vime quickly added. 'It's so nice to see you. I was hoping you'd be here.'

Looking a little mollified, the girl replied, 'I told you. I'm always here. I was angry with you for being late so I wasn't going to show myself. But Kijübode likes you and he thought I should answer your question.'

'Who's Kijübode?'

'The tree.'

'The tree has a name!'

'He has many names', the girl replied quite matter of fact, frowning disapprovingly, as if Vime ought to know this.

Vime's head was spinning. She wondered whether she was dreaming. Struggling to grasp indicators of reality, Vime looked down her favourite (and dirty) white canvas shoes, the clothes she was wearing (with the sleeves still damp from doing laundry), the arms of her jacket firmly tied around her waist. She looked at the footpath and the distant fields she had passed just a few moments past. If this is a dream, then surely all these little banal details wouldn't register in my head, I wouldn't even know how I got here,

Vime tried to make sense—trying to recall what she knew of the nature of dreams.

'You said the tree thought you should answer my question? What question?'

'Didn't you ask where you were?' the girl asked in exasperation, rolling her eyes exaggeratedly and making Vime feel extremely dull and stupid.

'Oh, right! I'm sorry, yes. So, what is this place?'

'This place is where the earth was birthed. And Kijübode is the portal between the human world and what lies beyond.'

FOUR

Vime struggled to stifle her laughter. She knew she wouldn't be able to stop if she gave in to the bubbling mirth threatening to spill over. However, the girl continued to look at her, straight-faced and expressionless, giving no indication that she had said anything out of the ordinary. She was certainly convincing. Vime was fascinated. She wondered if the girl was a bit touched in the head. Poor girl! She looked so normal; well, almost! But Vime enjoyed her company immensely and so she decided to play along. It had been awfully long since she could say that of anyone.

'Oh, I see. That's amazing! I'm Vime, by the way.'

'I know.'

'Don't be silly! How could you know?! And what's yours?'

The girl pursed her lips childishly and appeared in deep thought for a good second or two before she answered.

'Teikhrieruopfü!' she said with satisfaction, as if she had just decided on it. 'But you can call me Tei. And I'm not being silly. I've known your name for some time now.'

'Did you just make up your name?' Vime chuckled in delight, laughter spilling over her words, no longer bothering to suppress her amusement.

'No. I forget sometimes, that's all.'

'How can you forget your name?'

'It happens. You would forget your name, too, if nobody bothers to ask in a long time.'

What a funny girl! Vime thought inwardly but didn't say so. Instead, she asked again:

'How do you know my name?'

'I just do. You look like a Vime. But to be honest, I couldn't really make out until recently. I've seen a grainy visage of you wandering down the human path many times in the past—you were always absorbed with the things of your world and I knew you were beyond my reach then. But lately, you seemed to be drifting closer to my world. And so, I finally decided to try calling you. And it worked! You heard me today, didn't you?'

Before Vime could respond to the strangest explanation she had ever heard, Tei threw her head back and whistled. Suddenly, the forest was filled with the same song which had brought Vime to the forest. Softly resounding echoes of children's laughter amidst gushing water engulfed her like an orchestra of whispers. Vime felt herself transported to past happy memories which filled her with unbearable bittersweet sadness. The enchantment broke the moment Tei ended her song.

'What's made you so melancholic?' Tei asked.

'It's Apfo. She passed away the previous fall. I think about her all the time and I can't stop missing her. Sometimes I literally feel quite out of breath when

I think of her. It's like my body and mind are living separate realities.'

Vime had not confided this to anyone and she suddenly felt acutely aware that she was revealing her most intimate anguish to a complete stranger. But Tei answered with an understanding smile and reached out to squeeze her hand gently. The simple gesture comforted Vime, and she suddenly felt like Tei understood her better than the people she had known her entire life.

With an easy caprice which now felt familiar and quite characteristic, Tei tugged at Vime's hand and urged, 'Come with me!' Her melodic voice rang with merry mischief and excitement.

'Where? Is it far? I have to return home early. I almost got into trouble the last time', Vime's vacillation was weak as she was already allowing Tei to lead her.

'I promise you won't be late', Tei promised solemnly. Tei gave her word with such dignity that Vime believed her. As she enthusiastically nodded her consent, she felt little winged creatures of anticipation wildly fluttering in the pit of her stomach.

'Where are we going?' Vime asked as Tei carefully guided her around the tree with dainty little steps, deliberate and precise. They circled the tree thrice and by the completion of the third, Vime felt the bright mellow afternoon turn into a cool blue-green dusk, like an invisible hand had suddenly dimmed the lights. Soft clouds were lit pink and orange from within as if they had swallowed the sun.

Tei let go of her hand then and gestured welcome as a spellbound Vime found herself facing a vast valley with fields of muted gold amidst feathery catkins and willowy wildflowers. Shadowy outlines of cascading hills loomed behind while a bright luminous moon hovered above. The enormous moon hung invitingly low and Vime felt her breath catch as she resisted the instinctive urge to sprint towards the moon for a lunar embrace.

'What is this place? Am I in a dream?' Awestruck, Vime's gaze wandered everywhere. The surreal landscape was achingly beautiful and she felt her heart leap in exhilaration, sheer delight tinged with the bittersweet pang of nostalgia. This place was like the slow and tentative reawakening of a beautiful childhood memory, once cherished, now forgotten.

Tei laughed her forest laugh in response to Vime's wonderment and took hold of both Vime's hands in her own. With a delighted squeal, Tei whirled Vime round and round in dizzying circles until Vime felt her feet effortlessly lifted off the ground, oh so lightly. Hand in hand with Tei, Vime soared over high mountains and floating valleys, and great lakes of blue and silver. She felt a soft breeze against her face as they flew into the heart of the moon. Vime imagined she was the moon herself as its terrible loneliness resounded within her own. She wanted to stay but Tei was not done showing her around. Next, Vime found herself languorously gliding over the crest of a hill, so low that her hands brushed against the tips of blades of grass and softly scattered wildflowers. She felt invisible icy fingers nimbly tuck flowers in her hair.

Finally, the pair landed in the middle of a tidy little paddy field lined with fragrant guava trees around the edges. They were not alone. There were children, little girls, Vime presumed. Although they had their backs towards her,

each had long pitch-black hair reaching down their ankles.
They were plucking guavas and the smallest of them, being
shorter than the rest, kept jumping with arms outstretched
towards a low hanging branch weighed down by a delicious
profusion of fruits. As she paused to bend her knees before
another spirited little jump, Vime noticed that her feet were
inverted. 'Miawenuos!' Vime breathed out in astonishment.
She had heard so much about these diminutive and shy
female spirits with long hair and inverted feet. They were
rarely seen these days. 'They are not very bright and
understand things in reverse. Ask a Miawenuo for riches
and she will give you cow dung. But ask for cow dung
and she will grant you riches!' Atsa, grandmother, had once
explained. Atsa had told her that if she was ever fortunate
to come across a Miawenuo, she should not blink as these
spirits were notorious for vanishing within the blink of an
eye. As Vime looked on in fascination, a rustling sound
from the other direction had the tiny spirits scatter, fleeing
with shared mischievous glee and quickly vanishing behind
the grove of trees.

Vime turned her gaze towards the direction of the
sound and it was only then, that she noticed a prü located
on the adjacent terrace field. She could see inside, the
silhouette of a woman, squatting and blowing alive a fire.
The little prü and everything around it—the neat modest-
sized terraces, tickberry bushes with the memorable yellow
and orange flowers which Mother had taught her and
Neime to build into garlands, cosmos blooming alongside
the hedgerows, the steady low hum from the bamboo pipes
regulating the flow of water, the location of the guava trees,
the stream below, everything felt achingly familiar. This

time, Vime was absolutely convinced that she knew this place. Everything was just as she remembered, right where she knew where it'd be. She thought hard until astonished realization dawned. This field was exactly like the plot of the ancestral land her maternal grandparents owned. Her parents often took her and Neime to this field whenever they visited the village. Meanwhile, the woman inside the prü appeared to have finished whatever she was doing and wearily stretched her arms as she stepped outside, facing Vime. The woman looked directly at Vime but did not appear to see her.

'Apfo!' Vime unconsciously spoke aloud in utter shock and bewilderment. She felt a surge of electricity through the entire length of her body. It was Mother; only she looked younger and a lot slimmer. Feeling her knees grow weak and fluid, Vime slumped down the ground, tears streaming down her face. She wondered whether she was in heaven but she had no recollection of dying or of death.

She suddenly felt a strong grip on her shoulder. It was Tei.

'Vime, it's time to leave', the spirit said. Yes, Vime understood that Tei was a spirit now.

'No! That's Apfo, I have to go to her.'

'You can't. You don't belong here'.

Vime cried her protest and struggled to break free of Tei's unusually firm grip but the diminutive spirit effortlessly dragged her backwards with superhuman strength.

Vime woke, thrashing and weeping against the forest floor underneath the tree. The afternoon sun nonchalantly shone as if it had never gone down. She briefly felt the crushing disappointment of waking from a dream she was not ready to wake from. But as she recalled all that she had seen, she could not believe that she might have dreamt the entire thing. She had had many vivid dreams of Mother in the past and had woken, broken-hearted with the realization that Mother was still gone. But never a dream like this. As she continued to sob piteously, a wildflower fell into her hands from behind her ear. It was a tiny lavender flower with a bright yellow centre. Vime carefully placed the flower inside her pocket and got up in a daze.

'Tei!' she shouted over and over, circled the tree thrice and then once more. But there was no response—only the sound of the wind against the trees, insects mournfully wailing and the little stream trickling down below, calm and serene.

'Kijübode!' Vime looked up, facing the tree and declared boldly, 'Tei will not answer me. But you are here and I know you are listening. I want you to know that I'm going home. For now. But I'm coming back to this place where the earth was birthed.'

FIVE

'Vime, is that you?' Neimenuo called as she heard Vime noisily run up the stairs.

'Just a minute. I'll be right down', Vime exclaimed with feigned cheery insouciance, quickly escaping to her room and slamming the door.

After splashing cold water on her face, Vime anxiously searched her face in the mirror. Her fair skin still looked a little blotchy from having wept so hard earlier but she looked presentable enough, she decided in relief. She needed to gather her thoughts and make sense of everything that she had experienced. And she was not ready to share this with anyone.

Vime got on her knees and pulled out an old shoebox from under her bed, the cardboard edges soft and plaint with age. Inside were candy wrappers, colourful birthday and Christmas cards diligently collected over the years and finally, what she sought neatly tucked on the bottom, a journal with half the pages still unwritten. It had been Mother's final gift to her. Vime had stopped writing in it after Mother's demise. She gingerly took out the journal, opened a random page, and furiously began scribbling, almost as if she feared her memory might be compromised with each passing second.

'October 15', Vime began with the date as she had missed an entire year:

> I heard the forest singing and followed the cobbled footpath passing Aunty Sebu's house and past the kharü and also the fields till I reached a big old tree. I met the same girl I had encountered the last time I got lost in the forest. Her name is Tei and she told me the tree's name is Kijübode.
>
> Tei told me that the place where I stood was where the earth was birthed and that the tree is the gateway between the human world and what lies beyond. I didn't believe it but Tei took my hand and together, we circled the tree thrice. Tei led me to a beautiful valley where I saw Apfo. And forcefully brought me back before I could speak to her.

As she continued to write, hot tears spilled over, dissolving the fresh ink on paper, transforming letters into watery blue flowers. Vime roughly wiped her eyes with the back of her sleeves and added a quick postscript about first meeting Tei the night she got lost. She then took out the wildflower from inside her pocket and carefully tucked it within the pages. She noticed that although fragile-looking, the minuscule wildflower was resilient. Not a single petal had fallen loose.

Writing always helped Vime assess things more clearly. As she regained some degree of composure, she calmly debated telling Neime how she had seen their mother but decided against it as she ruminated over the possibilities of what might happen if she did confide in her family. Neime was sure to tell Father. What if they didn't believe her and thought she was making up stories? But then again, what if they did believe her? She might have to take them to the tree then. Tei was such a moody creature and Vime feared that Tei may not show up at all if she brought more people to the forest and she'd be left feeling desperately stupid. And then everybody would simply tell her she must have imagined the entire thing. 'The mind is a powerful thing!' she imagined Neime telling her in her newly acquired patronizing manner of speaking. There was also the likelihood that she may be forbidden to go to the forest thereafter. She would then never be able to see mother again. The last thought was unbearable. Vime felt like her solitary walks and this new discovery were the only things which made life worth living. No, I can't tell them, at least not right now, Vime decided, as she replayed her adventure in her mind.

Heavy pounding upon her door jolted Vime out of her reverie. It was Neime.

'What?!' Vime yelled irritably, feeling like she had no privacy in this house.

'Open the door, Vime.'

'Behave yourself!' Neime scolded, as Vime sulkily opened her door. 'Atsa Neidonuo and Ania Ataü are here, they've been here for a while now. Come down and say hello.'

Ania Ataü was Father's older sister. Atsa Neidonuo was a much older woman who took pride in her years as elderly people were wont to do. 'Remember, I have seen the moon before you', she would always remind Mother whenever she thought her age gave her advantage in their frequent disagreements. Regardless, Atsa Neidonuo and Mother had been good friends. Vime had always been a little wary of the cantankerous elderly woman who made it her business to know about everyone's business. 'Neimenuo has been raised well, so medie and well mannered! But you've certainly allowed this one to grow wild!' the elderly woman had once criticized, uncaring that Vime was within earshot. Atsa Neidonuo prided herself on her brutal honesty.

'Why do old people feel they've earned the right to say whatever they want?' Vime had grumbled to Mother later, which elicited the latter's distinctively deep-throated chuckles. Although Vime liked to act blasé, she always felt flattered that Mother found her funny. No one appreciated her remarks the way Mother did. And because perception becomes reality, Vime found that she was at her wittiest when she was with Mother. Mother had patiently explained, 'Ignore her remarks. She has a kind heart underneath the brusque exterior. Next time you meet her, make it a point to greet her first before she does you, and address her as "Atsa", not "Aunty". She puts great store in being cultured.'

This evening, however, much to Vime's relief, neither Atsa Neidonuo nor Ania Ataü paid much attention to her. After she greeted them, she served tea prepared by Neime and sat by the fireplace, unnecessarily stoking the fire now and then to ease her restlessness. The women stayed for dinner too. Father was less taciturn than usual and conversed with the women while they ate, and they all laughed an awful lot, Vime felt. Father looked a bit uncomfortable at times but perhaps that was because of Atsa Neidonuo's presence. During one of Atsa Neidonuo's long drawn-out monologues, Vime caught Father's eye and he gave her a conspiratorial wink which made her grin.

After a while, Vime left them as she didn't think they'd notice. That night, Vime dreamt of the enchanted valley and a youthful mother.

The next day, Vime was dismayed to find Father and Neime already home after she returned from school. Having started her first year at college, Neime usually returned later than Vime. To be safe, however, Vime had rushed home from school so that she could discretely leave for her secret spot. To her dismay, Father called her while she was trying to figure a way to keep her heavy school bag unseen and leave the house.

'Ah Vime! Come here, help your sister clean these dishes.' Father was taking out the good china which mother reserved only for special occasions.

'How are you home so early?' she asked.

Father raised his eyebrows and muttered something non-committal. Then he cleared his throat in an unusually diffident manner and explained that they would be having some visitors.

'Not sure whether they'll stay for dinner but anyway . . .', Father's voice trailed away. He appeared extremely nervous and clumsily dropped the same bowl twice while a suspicious Vime subjected him to intense scrutiny.

Apparently Atsa Neidonuo and Ania Ataü would be bringing along with them, two or three other guests.

'But why? They already visited yesterday!' Vime crossly remarked.

'Hush, n kethe, Vime, don't be rude', Neime chided.

The visitors ultimately did not stay for dinner but they had tea and Neimenuo's freshly fried nimki, crisp on the outside and soft inside, which everyone relished and praised in turn. There was a young woman who did not speak much but was pleasant towards Vime and Neimenuo. Her name was Khrieliezonuo and she stood out due to her pale complexion and vaguely Caucasian features.

Later, while washing the dishes together, Neime explained that Khrieliezonuo's father was a British soldier who had left Kohima after the war, promising to return for his wife and unborn child but never did. The two girls were alone in the house as Father had gone to drop the elderly Atsa Neidonuo.

'She's rather beautiful, isn't she? She has extremely sad eyes though. Maybe that's why', Vime reasoned.

'Did you like her?' Neime asked thoughtfully. Her question seemed loaded with meaning.

'She's alright, I guess. Why?'

'Listen, Vime. Father confided in me this morning. Apparently Atsa Neidonuo and Ania Ataü are suggesting that Father remarry. They think that Khrielie might be the one. Father isn't sure but agreed to meet her and see how we get along first. This was the purpose of tonight's gathering.' Neime's words rapidly gushed forth like she had been dying to tell Vime and was just waiting for the right time.

'Khrielie?! They can't be serious! Why, she's much too young for Father, it's ridiculous!' Vime exclaimed, although she really couldn't care less how old the woman was.

'I know. I was surprised, too. I suspected she'd be younger than Apfo, but I never imagined she'd be this young.'

Vime felt her heart plummet as Neime mentioned Mother. Even Neime appeared distressed as she unconsciously unrolled and twisted the damp kitchen towel around her fingers.

'How could Father do this to Apfo? It's too soon. We don't need a stranger in our lives.'

'It's alright. Father hasn't made any decision yet and I'm sure he won't, without consulting us. Let's not upset ourselves unnecessarily before talking to him.'

Father returned home to find his daughters waiting for him in the kitchen, stiffly seated by the edge of their seats, looking at him with anxious expressions. He took a deep breath but said nothing. Father had never been much of a talker. They looked at each other in silence, each waiting for the other to speak first.

Vime found the silence intolerable and blurted. 'Father, are you going to marry Khrieliezonuo?' Her tone sounded accusing although she had not intended to be so. His grim silence was more than she could bear and she burst into tears.

'Don't you like her? I thought you girls were getting on well!' Father's voice sounded almost pleading.

'She's so young! It's disgusting. What would Apfo say?' Vime exclaimed, her voice trembling with raw rioting emotions. She regretted her words the moment they came out but nevertheless, felt angry recklessness welling inside. Father had no business remarrying. She had unwittingly touched a raw nerve as Father's expression became so livid that Vime could see the prominent vein on his temple bulge and twitch.

'Father, what Vime means to say is that. . .', Neime began but Father abruptly cut her off.

'Enough. Both of you, go to your rooms now. This is not something you children will understand!' Father said tersely.

Neime opened her mouth to say something but Father simply strode to the kitchen, opened the little cabinet on top and poured himself a drink.

'Go to bed, both of you, we'll talk about this in the morning', Father bit out, his tone firmly conveying that this was the end of discussion. That night, Vime and Neime slept in the same bed—something they had not done for years now, hugging each other for comfort as they bleakly contemplated what the future would be like with a stepmother. Father had neither confirmed nor denied anything. Did that mean he had made up his mind to remarry? How mortifying if their father had a proper wedding; would Father and Khrielie have children of their own? Would she and Neime then become outsiders in their own house? Oh, Apfo! How could you leave us to this?

SIX

Father cradled his glass of tawny liquid and brooded late into the night. Finally, he got up to splash cold water on his face. It had a sobering effect and gave him clarity of thought. He regretted the way he had handled the conversation. He had never been a good communicator and had rehearsed what he would say on his way home. But everything had gone wrong the moment Vime brought their late mother into the conversation. The girl was too spirited for her own good; her mother has indulged her too much, he mulled in fresh irritation.

He had meant to ask their opinion of Khrieliezonuo first. Granted, she was young. But it wasn't like he was spoilt for choice. And despite his initial reservations, he found himself liking the girl. He knew he would be kind to her and could give her a comfortable life. His dutiful elder daughter Neimenuo was trying her best to maintain the house the way her late mother used to. But Neimenuo is a child herself, he thought, it wasn't fair that she should have to. Instead, his girls need a mother, he concluded, rather defensively. Truth may be, he was just so desperately lonely.

Father fought the impulse to knock on his daughters' door. It was late and they would be sleeping now. His wife would have known how to approach the girls. She had been so good with them and they adored her, going to her for everything; sometimes he had felt like an outsider and the three of them a happy little family all on their own. He regretted not forging a relationship with his daughters when they were younger. He had always wanted a boy. And when his wife gave birth to two daughters in turn, he had more or less relegated the task of bringing them up to her. And now with his wife gone, he did not know how to speak to his daughters.

And so, Father did the only thing he could. He called Ania Ataü, his elder sister.

Very soon hence, without further deliberations between father and daughters, it was established that father would and must remarry. His new wife and their new mother would be Khrieliezonuo.

'No, you don't have to call her mother if you don't want to', Ania Ataü reassured a relieved-looking Neime. It would be good for all of them, Ania Ataü persuaded; they could not do better than Khrielie. Snippets of conversation which Vime overheard in the ensuing days concerned the helplessness of widowers who were used to wives looking after them. Vime felt quite disgusted; she never imagined that men were so incapable of self-care. Vime wondered whether Ania and the other women were indirectly justifying father's remarriage for her benefit, but they didn't seem to notice her presence. Many of these statements were professed as general truths.

'Hou derei! Men are helpless creatures, increasingly as they get older. They need wives to tend to their needs.'

'His children need a mother.'

Vime listened, mutely indignant, as the womenfolk praised and criticized their own gender in turn, for any perceived shortcomings of the men.

'His shirt collar looked all frayed and worn. Disgraceful! I blame the wife.'

'Poor fellow! I can't understand why they haven't found him a wife yet! That is their sisterly duty.'

Ania Ataü seemed to have an inexhaustible list of such antiquated societal maxims in her discourse. Ania herself had been a widow for many years. Her husband had died of alcoholism. Vime remembered him as a genial man but Neime had once mentioned that their mother had never approved of Father spending too much time with their uncle because of his weakness for liquor and consequently, women. One Sunday afternoon, Vime asked, 'But Ania, what about you?'

Ania Ataü appeared nonplussed for a moment but quickly recovered, 'Oh! We women are different. We're more independent. We can occupy ourselves with housework the entire day.' Ania then leaned forward in a conspiratorial manner, 'You see, Vime, we are known as the weaker sex but we're emotionally much stronger than men.' She finished with a triumphant, childishly smug look but Vime was not entirely convinced. She wondered whether her aunt ever felt lonely too. But it was a fleeting thought which vanished quickly as Ania Ataü's expression suddenly turned steely. The woman turned her seat to face Vime square in the eyes and spoke.

'Vime, as you know, I am your father's older sister. Therefore, I feel it is my duty to tell you this especially now that your dear mother, God rest her soul, is not here to guide you. You are not a child anymore and so you have to learn to use your words wisely. Not recklessly like an immature child throwing tantrums whenever things don't go your way. You know, your father was very hurt with your words that night. Try to be more careful and ladylike—just like your sister Neime.'

Vime felt her face burn with furious resentment and humiliation. Most of her anger was directed towards Father for telling on her, to Ania Ataü, of all people! Vime considered her aunt to be one of the most judgmental people she knew, with Atsa Neidonuo a close second. As she stared mute and speechless, repressing a heated retort, Ania Ataü patted her lap in a placating manner and said, 'Please believe me when I say that I mean this with love.'

Alone in her room that night, Vime miserably scribbled down the latest developments of her young life inside her journal. The more she narrated her woes, the more justified she felt and her despondency grew. There must be a way out, she contemplated desperately. She was also upset that she had lost an ally in Neime who, Vime felt, had reconciled to Father's impending remarriage too quickly. But then again, it would not be so difficult for Neime to adjust, Vime decided ruefully. Her sister got on well with most people and was generally well liked. It was she, Vime, who was the misfit, the oddball.

'I wish I was with Mother, instead. I don't belong here', Vime voiced out bitterly. She felt her heart lurch fearfully, as if the organ knew, even if she did not, that she ought not to give voice to such thoughts. The wildflower neatly tucked within the bared pages fluttered, although there was no breeze inside the room. Vime curiously got up to check whether the windows were open but seeing that it was securely latched, sat back down. She thought of Mother still in that field in the enchanted valley and wished with all her heart that she was there too. The turn of events had delayed her planned foray into the woods to seek out Tei and the earth's birthplace wherein lies the ultimate gateway in the form of the tree Kijübode. Melancholy determined that nothing would hold her back now. As Vime drifted to sleep that night, she comforted herself with the knowledge that she would soon be escaping to a land only she knew existed.

SEVEN

Like the many mornings past, Vime woke to an empty house. Father who had a relatively long commute had already left for work and Neime had early morning tuitions. The hearth was still alive with smoldering coals, while tongues of red flames licked the ancient charred and soot-blackened kettle. Vime pensively stared at the ashes. She had heard that in the old days, bereaved families who had lost a loved one would spread ashes on the floor and leave the door half open. Footprints upon the ashes in the morning would convey that the soul of the deceased missed them in return. A glum Vime impatiently disturbed the ashes and coals with the fire tongs, sending smoky ash and fiery little sparks up the air.

Vime grunted with the weight of the kettle as she poured scorching hot water from the kettle for a bath. The empty kettle hissed as she absent-mindedly put it back over the fire. On the dining table was her sunny-yellow tiffin which Neime had packed before leaving. Other times, when Neime was too rushed to prepare lunch, she would keep some lunch money aside for Vime. There was a note on top of the tiffin box, reminding Vime to refill the kettle after use and to put out the fire before leaving for school. Vime was running late for school but it didn't matter because she had other plans today.

Sitting by the fire, a lonely Vime quietly ate her meant-for-school tiffin meal of white boiled rice and crusty potato wedges while the hot water inside the bucket quickly grew lukewarm under the late autumn chill.

Vime listlessly wandered the house, finally ending up in her sister's girly room. She dispassionately inspected the sparkly little trinkets and cosmetics, carefully laid out on Neime's dressing table. Neime's room was as feminine as her, and Vime felt quite out of place. She had no interest in things that girls were generally supposed to like.

'Oh, that's because you're still young. Give it a few years and you'll be as vain as your sister', Mother had once gaily predicted, making Vime wonder whether all girls were expected to grow into copies of each other—wanting, needing the same things.

Vime waited a while, hoping that everyone in the neighborhood had left for the day's work before heading to the forest. She really didn't want to bump into anyone midway. She picked up the Enid Blyton book that she had been struggling to finish since the past few days and restlessly put it away for the umpteenth time, not bothering to mark the book. Vime used to love reading but of late, she found that no story could sustain her attention for long. This worried her sometimes—that perhaps something alive in her had died along with Mother. One particularly bleak night, Vime imagined herself a candle whose flickering flame would not last the long night. She found she no longer cared about things the way she used to—books and music, school; they meant little now. Little irritations were all she felt. There was a shocked numbness which had settled deep within and she could not shake it off.

Soon, Vime found herself seeking the comfort of her beloved cobbled footpath and the wondrous secrets it held. Knowing she had the whole day to herself, Vime leisurely entertained herself by gingerly stepping upon the cobblestones only, avoiding the crevices and spaces in between. With each step she took, she experienced a sense of belonging, feeling that this was right where she was meant to be.

'Tei, I'm back', Vime expectantly called out the moment her foot landed upon the final step. It was a crisp clear morning and the forest sounded bright and alive, buzzing with typical forest sounds. Only Kijübode appeared regal and otherworldly while everything else appeared almost, well, normal. But there was no sign of Tei anywhere. Disheartened, Vime sat herself down. As she anxiously continued to wait for Tei, she regretted that she had not had the sense to bring her book and maybe something to eat while waiting. I shouldn't have eaten my tiffin, I wasn't even hungry then, Vime ruefully thought to herself. She had not anticipated that Tei may not show. Determined not to give up, however, Vime entertained herself by hunting for what she considered uniquely shaped pebbles in the stream below when her ears suddenly perked as she heard footsteps and the humming of an unfamiliar melody. The sound came from above the stream. Abandoning her neat little treasure of pebbles, Vime eagerly scrambled up the slope and to her disappointment, came face to face not with Tei, but a woman who looked just as surprised to see her. She lugged a khorü on her back, filled to the brim with forest vegetables. The woman promptly broke into relieved laughter.

'Goodness me! You startled me! I thought a wild animal was charging.'

Disappointment rendered Vime speechless. The woman was a friendly sort and continued her banter, undeterred, 'What are you doing here all alone?'

'Oh. I'm waiting for a friend', Vime replied. She didn't think it was a lie.

'Whose child are you? Shouldn't you be in school during this time?' demanded the woman, her tone evocative of the friendly nosiness of small-town folk.

'I decided not to go today', Vime answered truthfully.

The woman frowned, looking concerned and skeptical all at once. She raised her eyebrows but didn't say anything. She looked as if she wanted to say something further but held back. Instead, she said after a lengthy pause;

'Well, Neinuo, I think you'd better head back home now. The nights are increasingly eating into daylight. It'll be getting dark very soon and let me tell you, these forests are not half as delightful after dark.'

'Why do you say that?'

'These are old forests; hidden beings abound after dark.'

Vime's dark eyes sparkled with curiosity and this pleased the woman. She leaned forward conspiratorially as she spoke, 'When I was a child, I would look down here from a vantage point on top of that hill . . . ', her hands occupied with the khorü straps, the woman tossed her head upwards to point out the location before she continued, 'And often, I would see naked little children dancing around this tree. Imagine! Being a child myself then, I thought nothing of it. I haven't seen them for the longest time now', the woman finished, rather regretfully.

'Do you come here often?' Vime asked.

'Quite often, yes.'

'Have you ever seen a girl my age around this area?'

'No. I can't say I have', the woman replied slowly, trying to recollect as she spoke.

'Oh. Well . . . I'll go home soon, I promise', Vime said disappointedly, bringing the conversation to an abrupt close.

After giving Vime a final curious look, the woman continued on her way, humming as she trudged onwards with her khorü resting heavy against her back.

Vime thoughtfully continued to watch the woman's retreating figure until she heard a familiar voice:

'I'm glad you didn't let her persuade you to leave.'

The unmistakable sound of Tei's sweetly melodic voice filled Vime with a heady sense of relief. Everything would be alright now, she thought.

EIGHT

The diminutive elfin spirit was sitting cross-legged beneath the tree, looking bored and most humanlike. Tei looked at Vime impassively as if she had been sitting there all along.

'Tei, I thought you'd never show! Where were you?'

'Right here. Didn't I tell you that I'm always here?'

'No, you weren't. I searched for you everywhere and I didn't see you', Vime replied, feeling quite annoyed.

'Humans!' Tei muttered curtly, her tone scathing, 'Listen. Just because you can't see me doesn't mean I'm not here. I wanted to see what you'd do.'

'Well, I waited. I wasn't going to leave without seeing you. Tei, the woman said she's been here often but has never seen you. Why's that? Are you invisible to adults?' Vime asked, wonder in her voice, daring to feel special.

'No, Vime, I am most certainly not invisible to adults', Tei peevishly replied, enunciating each word in a mocking staccato manner and not bothering to answer her question.

Vime had been angry with Tei for preventing her from talking to her mother and she had half expected Tei to be the one trying to mend their friendship. But now, seeing Tei behaving so detached and rude, she felt confused hurt building.

'Tei, why did you stop me from going to Apfo? Where was that place you took me to?'

'I told you why. You are a living human. You weren't supposed to be there in the first place. It is forbidden to reveal oneself to the souls of the departed.'

'But why? What would happen if I did?'

Tei got up impatiently, leaping to her feet in one fluid unnatural movement, not bothering to reply. Worried that Tei might disappear if she pressed too much, Vime changed tactics by asking less confrontational questions.

'Please don't be angry, Tei', she tried to appease a surly looking Tei. 'I'm just really puzzled. Where was that place you took me to? It was the most beautiful place I've ever seen in my entire life.'

Looking a tad appeased, Tei answered, 'Remember when I told you that this tree is the gateway between the human and spirit world? Well, I couldn't take a human to the spirit world. The keepers of the forest would never allow it. But I was able to take you to the fringes bordering the human and spirit world. We call it the in-between. That's where human souls stop to rest before their final journey to paradise. And that's where you saw your mother.'

'Was it really her? She looked different.'

'I don't know. The beings and places found in the fringes of the two worlds are a mystery for us spirits, too.

The in-between is ever changing; coalescing, expanding outward, inward, evanescing . . .', Tei's voice trailed off.

'Tei, please help me meet Apfo again. I will do anything you ask', Vime felt her heart thump as she said the words.

Tei's eyes gleamed suddenly and she looked at Vime as if she was the most interesting thing she had ever set eyes upon. The spirit looked bright-eyed and alert now, all trace of boredom gone.

'Well, no one has ever attempted to meet the souls in the in-between. Not even spirits. But seeing as you are my friend . . . perhaps I can try.'

'Oh, would you? I would be eternally grateful to you', Vime burst out, hope filling her heart with elation.

'Hmph! The gratitude of humans means naught to us spirits', Tei spat disdainfully, once again revealing her temperamental lightning change of moods. 'You have to promise me something in return, instead.'

'Anything.'

'Promise you will allow me to bind a part of your soul to my forest song, in exchange.'

'What does that mean?'

'Oh, it's nothing really; the smallest favour considering I'm about to break a kenyü by helping you' Tei stated ominously, the word kenyü delicately rolling off her tongue slowly and with meaning.

Vime felt her throat tighten with nervousness and she swallowed audibly. She had heard of the different kinds of taboos known as kenyü and how it was simply forbidden to break them. The repercussions could be devastating.

Satisfied with Vime's reaction, Tei continued airily, 'It simply means a little part of you will reside within my song. You'd have the best of both worlds really—half in the human world and half in the spirit world.

Vime restlessly shifted from one foot to the other. She felt uneasy and fairly certain it might mean more than that. She wished Neime was here to consult with. As annoying as her elder sister could be, Vime had to concede that Neime gave good advice when asked for.

'I don't know, Tei, I don't understand. Can people live with half a soul?' Vime asked, not even sure where to begin addressing her confusion.

'Tchh!' Tei snarled like a cat, her eyes turning into angry slits. For the first time, Vime felt scared of Tei. 'Silly human girl! Who said anything about half a soul? You would be whole, just residing in two homes instead of one.'

'Why do you want me in your forest song?' Vime persisted.

Tei took a deep dramatic breath and went silent, her sharp little features now crimson with temper and dreadfully contorted. As seconds ticked by without a single word from Tei, Vime almost began to wish that she had left before Tei showed herself. The woman she met was right. The forest did not look as inviting in the late hours. Early dusk had begun to set and a wraithlike mist shrouded the woods like a thin muslin cloak, swirling up and around the magnificent Kijübode, almost as if it stemmed from the tree. It suddenly dawned on Vime that there was an unnatural stillness about the atmosphere. She strained her ears for sounds of birds chirping and the familiar cries of forest creatures but she could only hear the uneasy beating of her heart. Vime wondered whether she could slip away without Tei noticing.

Tei spoke just then, almost as if she could hear Vime's thoughts, 'So be it. I was trying to help you, ungrateful human girl. You had your chance and you did not take it. You can never see your mother again ever. Nor will you ever see me henceforth.' Saying this, Tei vanished within the blink of an eye just like the miawenos that Vime had heard about.

'No No No, Tei Tei! I'm sorry, please come back', Vime cried, suddenly gripped with alarmed panic. She should have jumped at the chance; she couldn't bear the thought of never seeing Mother ever. She ran back and forth, around the tree, desperately searching for Tei but there was not a trace of her.

'Tei, Tei, please come back!' Vime shouted over and over until the forest was filled with her pleading echoes.

After what seemed like forever, Vime finally gave up calling and searching for Tei. She slumped down the forest floor in anguished despair.

'Tei, please come back. I'm sorry. I'll do whatever you want me to if you help me meet Mother. I promise. You can take me for your forest song. Anything', Vime whispered softly, to herself really, her words careless and broken by sobs. The moment these words were uttered, she felt a stiff breeze pierce through her chest, if such a thing was possible. For the briefest moment, her insides felt cold as ice, but the chill passed as soon as it came. Tei was the wind, quietly listening and Vime's words had reawakened an old magic. But poor Vime did not know this.

Ennui seeped in, Vime felt her body grow sluggish as she heavily dragged herself from up the forest floor. There was no sign of Tei and it was getting late; time to go home.

Night crickets and fireflies chirped and buzzed as Vime listlessly dragged herself home. She felt eyes upon her all the way till she reached the old kharü.

NINE

Vime spent restless nights agonizing over Tei's condition. I wonder why Tei wanted me to do that anyway, would it make her song sweeter? She curiously wondered more than once, her insides churning with anxiety whenever Tei came to mind. Even she knew better than to make such a disquieting pledge. Nevertheless, she remained conflicted and sadness made her reckless. Vime had not been down the cobbled path since her last meeting with the elfin spirit but she incessantly ruminated back and forth, torn, her head and heart miles apart. A thick gloom of heartsick melancholy seized Vime during each nightfall's loneliness.

Last night, Vime had sporadic spells of sleep, feverishly tossing and turning in bed until the crowing of the rooster finally heralded dawn. Tei and her song had seemed a ubiquitous presence, like a pesky bee buzzing around her head, refusing to leave. Despite having slept little, Vime got up immediately, anxious to forget bad dreams. Mercifully, morning did bring some respite, chasing away Vime's morbid thoughts along with the darkness.

After washing her face with icy cold spring water, Vime looked at herself in the bathroom mirror, eyes steely, stubborn, determined. She could do this, she could find a way to visit the in-between, without giving in to Tei; it really didn't have to be so complicated. Vime screwed her forehead, wracked in deep thought. There must be another way. How many times had Mother called Vime her clever girl? Surely, she could convince Tei to agree to something else. She simply had to think of something, something Tei would want bad enough. Until then, Vime prudently decided not to visit the woods.

One good thing about father's impending remarriage was that it distracted Vime from brooding endlessly. Considering that this was to be father's second marriage, the conservative matchmakers had arrived at the consensus that the usual wedding festivities could be done away with. Ania Ataü relayed this news to a relieved Vime with an air of magnanimity, making it indisputably evident that she was behind this decision. Conventional wisdom cautioned that unnecessary delay gave rise to gossip and second thoughts. Very soon then, under the cover of night a fortnight from now, Khrielie's family would bring her to her new home. In light of what would soon be, there was a palpable atmosphere of nervous excitement in the house, much to Vime's disgust; she impatiently wondered whether it might be the same at Khrielie's house.

This afternoon, as Vime walked past Neime's room, she heard stereo music intermittently drowned by frequent squeals of girlish laughter and animated chatter. It was a

Saturday and her sister's friends were visiting. Vime found her father outside their porch, sitting on his haunches and polishing his good pair of shoes.

'Where are you going?' she asked

Father brought to halt the brisk activity and stopped to look at her thoughtfully. Slowly resuming to polish the shoe in his hand, he replied in a cautious tone which bordered on the defensive; 'Well Vime, seeing as I haven't visited Khrielie even once, I thought I would do that today . . . Would you like to come with me?' The invitation was hesitant.

Vime's first instinct was to decline but she suddenly thought of being home with Neime and her annoying friends and changed her mind; 'Alright. I think I will.' Father's face lit up when she agreed to come with him and it made her feel a little guilty.

'Go and get ready then, put on something warm now', Father urged, looking as pleased as a little boy with a shiny new toy.

'You're really accompanying Father?' Neime asked, her arms folded and looking absolutely staggered when she came across Vime in the hallway, all tidied up to go out with Father.

'Oh, hello Vime, you look so pretty today', Jabu, Neime's friend, exclaimed from inside the open room. She was comfortably lying on her stomach on the bed, propped by elbows. The rest of the girls simpered and all of a sudden, burst into delighted laughter over something which Vime did not care to know. Vime scowled, ignoring Neime and her friends as she joined Father who was waiting outside. Vime did not consider herself pretty, at least not like

Neime, and she did not appreciate anyone saying so. She only tolerated Mother saying such things because Mother was biased, bless her.

Khrielie's house was a lot more modest and unassuming than Vime had imagined. She lived with her mother and grandparents. Vime thought Khrielie's mother looked like someone who had once been very beautiful. Khrielie was preparing to bake a cake when the pair visited and she looked a tad flustered as she attempted to shake the powdery white flour off her dress and in the process, spread it even more.

'Don't mind me. Please, carry on', Father said apologetically. Vime realized their visit was unanticipated.

Vime had never seen a cake being baked and she promptly nodded when Khrielie's mother suggested that she help with the cake while Father conversed with Khrielie's family inside their pretty living room. Soon, Vime found herself in the kitchen helping to whip the batter. To bake the cake, Khrielie took out an old ammunition box. As Vime inspected the curious contraption, Khrielie explained that many such ammunition boxes had been left behind by British troops after the war and local bakers had ingeniously repurposed them as ovens. Seeing that she had piqued Vime's interest, Khrielie became increasingly eloquent.

'Another popular technique is to put sand in a big old pot and heat it over wood fire. The cake batter will be placed inside a smaller pot and placed atop the sand-filled pot, deftly inserted inside the sand, deep but not too deep so as to ensure that there is still enough sand at the bottom to prevent the cake from burning. These days, though, some bakers are using electric ovens sold in the Indian Army canteen.'

'How much do electric ovens cost?' Vime asked, idly curious.

Khrielie smiled, 'I'll let you know after I find out myself.'

When the cake was finally done, Khrielie deftly cut the cake into generous slabs and invited Vime to sample the first piece. Vime wrinkled her nose, a little skeptical seeing that the cake had sunken a little in the middle but to her pleasant surprise, she had to admit that it was the best she'd ever had. Soon, everyone was enjoying tea with fragrant butter cake. With Vime conspicuously seated between, Father and Khrielie made polite and somewhat stilted conversation.

Feeling restless suddenly, Vime got up to look outside the window. She shouldn't be wasting her time like this, she thought. She had to think of a plan soon before Tei gives up on her completely. Vime wasn't alone for long because Khrielie joined her shortly.

'I hope you're not too bored?' Khrielie asked. Vime glumly shook her head unconvincingly and deigned to sit beside Khrielie on a wooden bench, propped against the window.

'So how do you usually spend your weekends?' asked Khrielie.

'I like to explore the woods.'

Khrielie felt encouraged. She had half expected a monosyllabic mumbled response. Although Vime was unaware, Atsa Neidonuo had confided to Khrielie that the young girl was struggling to reconcile to her father's imminent remarriage. But it wasn't solely for this reason that she felt compelled to pay extra attention to the girl. For some inexplicable reason, Khrielie found herself drawn to Vime. Something in her gravitated towards this quiet, sullen-faced girl whose clear brown eyes held myriad emotions.

'That's nice. I used to explore the woods myself when I was younger. Back then, Mother and I used to live by ourselves in a little house not so far from yours. There was a secret place only I knew. Have you been down the old cobbled walkway which goes past the kharü? I'm sure you have.'

A thrill ran through Vime's spine and she stared straight into Khrielie's face, 'Yes, that's my favourite place to go. What was your secret place?'

'Oh, it was a little stream beside a huge tree. I used to pretend it was a vast ocean like the ones I'd seen in storybooks and spent many afternoons there, floating paper boats.'

Vime's heart calmed. So Khrielie had not seen Tei nor been to the in-between. But she had to be sure. 'What kind of tree, how did you find it? Was it right at the dead end of the footpath?'

'I'm sorry, Vime. I don't remember the exact route now. I do remember coming across the tree while collecting firewood by the edge of the woods. I was quite taken with how big and magnificent it looked', Khrielie answered with a fond smile, as if the tree was an old friend she had once known.

'Do you still go?'

'No. That was a long time ago'. There was an unnatural intensity in Vime's dark eyes which unnerved Khrielie. It was almost as if she was looking into the face of her own restless younger self. Khrielie leaned to pick the platter of cakes on the table.

'More cake?'

'Why not?' Vime persisted even as she accepted a piece of cake. Khrielie was saved from answering because they were interrupted by a beaming father who announced that they were in danger of overstaying their welcome and that it was time they took their leave. As he did so, Khrielie's mother promptly popped inside the kitchen and packed the remainder of the cake inside a little tin foil for Vime.

'Asshh this is quite unnecessary; Vime say thank you', Father exclaimed happily as Vime accepted the gift without hesitation.

Khrielie walked the pair outside while Vime impatiently sprinted ahead. Father was in a genial mood as they continued home.

'We stayed much longer than I anticipated. You didn't get too bored, did you?'

'No, I didn't.'

Before reaching the bend, Vime turned twice to look at Khrielie. Later, as Khrielie returned to the house, her mind lingered not on her fiancé but the curiously inscrutable expression etched on his daughter's face.

TEN

When Khrielie re-entered the house, she found her mother and grandparents still in the sitting room, discussing not Toulie, but his daughter Vime.

'Sweet-looking girl, somewhat dull though, isn't she? Didn't seem to want to talk much', her mother observed, still peering out the window although the father–daughter pair were long out of sight.

'What's her elder sister's name again? I keep forgetting', asked Khrielie's grandmother as she idly picked crumbs off the table with a finger.

'Neime. Vime and Neime, easier to remember their names together', Khrielie's mother touted and then unnecessarily added, 'Neime is the prettier of the two, beautiful manners too. Vime is a little rough around the edges, poor thing.'

'Mother, Vime is still a child!' Khrielie defended, looking quite severe and promptly hushing her mother thus. As she spoke, the realization that Vime would soon be not simply a child but *her* child dawned and the thought startled her. She was going to become a wife and mother all at once. She knew how Vime felt about the soon-to-occur transition and she understood. She wondered what Neime's feelings might be, underneath the facade of perfect manners.

Lost in thoughts, Khrielie pensively went about hauling in fresh rainwater from the water syntax outside and refilled the large empty jerrycan inside the neat and spacious kitchen. As she proceeded to wash the teacups, Mother interrupted her wandering thoughts, 'Have you taken hot water to your grandparents for their baths?' The elderly couple had become completely dependent upon the mother–daughter duo in their old age.

The family of four had now fallen into a comfortably predictable daily routine wherein after their morning meal, each would go about their own business until evening, when everyone would once again gather round the hearth for dinner and, thereafter, sit in companiable silence until bedtime.

It had not always been this idyllic. Until a few years ago, Khrielie and her mother lived by themselves in a little three-roomed cottage. It had always been just the two of them. With time, Khrielie had learned a sketchy sense of their story by piecing together little bits of history garnered from relatives, friends, neighbours and from her mother, often grudgingly, unwittingly rather, most times. For the longest time, her mother tried to impress upon a young Khrielie that the past was not up for discussion but really, they would both soon learn that no topic was considered off-limits in small communities or for that matter, any lived community. Unpleasant remarks about her mother were sometimes carelessly and cruelly tossed into earshot but more often than not, it was just plain tactlessness.

Khrielie learned that their once-modest accommodation had been begrudgingly allotted to her parents by Grandfather, who had disowned his daughter after she had gotten pregnant out of wedlock by her British soldier lover. Grandfather had apparently been livid and refused to allow them to live under the same roof in the family house. Khrielie still found it as much hurtful, as it was difficult, to believe that that her now-amiable grandfather could have been so harsh once. Her grandfather had been an active member of a union who had long vocalized the need for Nagas to be free from colonial rule. Neighbours still spoke about how he had thundered, 'You have besmirched my good name and brought shame to this family', when his wife brought their unusually timid daughter to him and broke the news of their daughter's delicate predicament. It was the stuff of legend. In the end, however, everyone felt the only practical solution was to gain a modicum of respectability by marrying the couple. The young couple lived together erratically for a brief period until the baby's father finally received his transfer orders to return to England as the war had come to an end. He had promised to return for his wife and unborn child but they never saw him again. Khrielie was born soon after. An infant Khrielie and her all-too-young mother continued to live alone, cut off from the rest of the family, for a long time. It was only in recent years, with the healing nature of time and other family members' intervention, that Khrielie and her mother completed the slow reconciliation by moving back into her grandparents' house. It just made better sense for everyone.

Nevertheless, the past remained a living breathing thing for Khrielie. She knew that she would never forget those colourless years when she would wake in the middle of the night to find her mother weeping piteously, uncaring that her young impressionable daughter laid beside her. On such nights, although her mother's warm body was next to hers, Khrielie felt convinced that she was all alone in the world. Her mother just seemed out of reach somehow, too far away, engulfed in her own secret despair. In later years, Khrielie would sometimes wonder whether her mother knew she had heard. She doubted it. Mother had been in another world then. They had never spoken of those bleak long nights.

Dull memories of mother's terrible loneliness had made Khrielie extremely protective of her mother, and she had a tendency to mother her own mother. This, therefore, made her always accommodating of the latter when she made indiscreet or careless remarks as she was often wont to do these days, like she did about Vime earlier.

Once again, Khrielie marvelled how Vime reminded her so much of her lost younger self, especially at that very moment when Vime had revealed how she enjoyed exploring the woods. Khrielie wondrously recalled how the young girl had seemed to come unnaturally alive when told about the tree beside the stream. Khrielie had not thought of the forest in a long time. Until now. Vime had so artlessly brought to life long-buried memories.

As she proceeded to clean off fallen leaves from the yard, Khrielie mused how she and Mother, too, had come a long way. She thought of her secret place, freshly ignited by Vime's unusual interest. Back then, the tree with the little stream alongside had seemed a place of refuge and she had spent many innocent solitary hours there, playing with imaginary friends who never inquired about her absent father and launched many pretty paper boats whenever she got bored. For some reason, Khrielie never felt lonely at that seemingly magical place. In fact, she would very often feel unseen eyes on her although she had never seen anyone aside from the usual birds and animals. Khrielie's play-pretend adventures near the tree almost always involved her mother being happy and gay, with no reason to weep in the dead of night. This was all she had ever wanted as a child, sensitive soul that she was. She had little dreams for herself alone.

Khrielie was unaware that back then, she had actually begun to alarm her mother with her penchant for slipping off alone. Not knowing her daughter's whereabouts, Khrielie's mother had worried about her daughter's activities, remembering her own clandestine liaisons another life ago which had irrevocably changed her life forever. However, even before she had the chance to discretely track her daughter's movements, Khrielie stopped leaving the house of her own accord. Not daring to express her deepest fears, Khrielie's mother quietly observed her daughter. Obviously, nothing untoward happened in the following months— no suspicious weight gain or signs of morning sickness. Nevertheless, it took months of dreadful suspense for something she dared not voice out loud, until Khrielie's mother could finally allow herself to breathe a sigh of relief. Khrielie was, of course, oblivious to her mother's needless worry. She had simply outgrown fantasies, outgrown her secret place.

As Khrielie mindlessly continued to sweep the already spotless yard for the umpteenth time, she recalled how strangely animated Vime had seemed when they had spoken of the forest. It made her uncomfortable although she couldn't understand why it should. She felt herself shudder involuntarily and tried to shake it off by going inside and joining her family around the kitchen hearth.

It was getting late. Night sounds swelled the air as the dying fire valiantly burned its final swansong. Grandfather had been reading a book in his armchair beside the fireplace. By now, however, it was evident that he had dozed off as his opened book rested face down upon his bulging well-fed stomach. The women exchanged grins as Grandfather suddenly began snoring with utter abandon.

'Come on now, old man, time for bed', Grandmother called out while Khrielie gently nudged her grandfather awake whilst lifting the book off him, carefully folding the tip of the opened page to mark the book. He allowed Khrielie's mother to support him as he gripped his walking stick with the other hand. Once a strong and proud man, age had mellowed both his spirit and body.

Mother returned to the kitchen after seeing to her parents. Khrielie was clearing away the remnants of the dinner they had shared.

'Khrielie, go to bed, it's getting late. You must get a good night's sleep and look presentable for any unexpected visitor tomorrow. Tiredness has made you look almost haggard. Why, I can see your eye bags', Mother chided happily.

'Yes, Mother', Khrielie responded, not minding the unflattering observation. It had been a long day and she really was exhausted. Ever since the marriage was

finalized, their house had been sporadically graced by the
odd visitor; relatives, curious neighbours and well-wishers
alike. Khrielie wryly thought that her mother was having
the best time of them all with her forthcoming nuptials,
playing the part of the most gracious of hostesses, which
came to her quite naturally too. Her mother was just that
kind of woman, forever childlike and coquettish, a child of
a woman who had repressed her intrinsically free-spirited
sociable nature for too long and was finally revelling in the
liberating pleasure of entertaining.

As Khrielie's weary head finally touched the pillow that
night, she half dreamt and thought of Vime once more,
standing alongside the tree with a little stream running
through. There was a shadow lurking in the background,
someone or something else; she could sense it. But sleepy
fatigue overcame curiosity and soon, Khrielie was sleeping
the dreamless soundless slumber of the innocent.

ELEVEN

Vime hastily tucked her journal underneath the mattress as Neime barged in without warning. It was late. Her friends had finally left.

'Can't you knock first?' Vime complained. She had been writing, lying stomach down in bed.

'Oh, sorry, Madam. What were you writing?' Neime asked unrepentant as she comfortably plopped herself on the edge of Vime's bed.

'Nothing . . .', Vime began and then suddenly felt quite suspicious, considering she had been out the entire day while Neime had been home, 'Did you read my journal?'

Neime rolled her eyes exaggeratedly, 'No one's interested in reading your journal, Vime. What do you have to write so much about anyway; you rarely do anything, go anywhere these days.'

Neime's response elicited a smug ear-to-ear grin upon Vime's face, which made Neime shake her head in amused disbelief. What an odd thing her little sister could be, she thought, what went on inside her head? If only she knew.

Neime asked, 'So how was your visit. Father seems quite pleased you went.'

'It was alright, I guess', Vime mumbled, looking down the floor, her arms hanging limp.

'You're so funny. I really don't understand you sometimes; I never thought you'd go voluntarily.'

Vime shrugged, 'I helped Khrielie bake a butter cake. It was really delicious, the best I ever had, better than Aunty Sebu's. Khrielie's mother packed the leftover slices for me. Try it, it's on the kitchen counter.'

'Hou derei! So, they've won you over with cake then.'

'Moto! I didn't say that', Vime quickly retorted. Her spirited rebuttal made Neime burst into laughter. Vime smiled sheepishly, understanding that Neime was only teasing. In no hurry to leave, Neime shook off her sandals and sat herself comfortably on the bed, cross-legged, compelling Vime to give her one of the two pillows she was using.

'Jabu said Khrielie is a wonderful homemaker. We have to clean the house properly before she comes.'

'How does Jabu know Khrielie?' Vime asked, thinking it curious how Neime's friend Jabu seemed to know everyone.

'She doesn't. But apparently her mother is always full of praises for Khrielie and has given her stamp of approval. You see, Vime, men are the deciders in important political matters but women rule social life', Neime ended quite importantly, repeating something she had heard another aunt say, leaving Vime quite impressed although she didn't say so.

'What is their house like? Is it better than ours?' Neime asked with the curiosity of a girl who had taken over the responsibility of maintaining a house, all too young. Her eyes hovered over and around Vime's room as she spoke, trying to view the room with the eyes of a visitor.

'It's very tidy but much smaller than ours. But their kitchen is larger and wonderfully stocked with a lot more food items and utensils. We baked a cake using an old ammunition box like the one Aunty Sebu has, but Khrielie said some bakers are using electric ovens now', Vime explained, her mind still lingering on the delicious cake.

'Remember the time Mother tried to bake a cake using the big old pot? What a disaster that was', Neime guffawed the words.

The two sisters giggled over the shared hilarious memory of their mother's spirited efforts and how she had tried to hide the ruined blackened pot from their father afterwards. Mother had been so much fun, always ready to try new things. This was nice, Vime thought, as they continued to reminisce after the laughter died. Neime and she rarely talked like this.

'Khrielie seems alright now, but what do you think she'll be like as a stepmother? It's such a horrid word, isn't it? Stepmother', Vime asked, wonderingly, distastefully.

'I'm sure she won't change too much. But if things ever get unbearable, we can always turn into hornbills and fly far far away', Neime remarked, her slim tapered fingers lightly fluttering the air, imitating flight. She was lying down sideways, facing Vime. Neime tried to sound flippant but her eyes suspiciously glistened.

'Turn into birds? What do you mean?' Vime asked, her forehead childishly screwed in curiosity. She had seen hornbills in flight in the forest a few times and found them quite stunning with their dramatically curved bill and regal plumes.

'Don't you remember the story about the girl who turned herself into a bird? Weren't you listening when Apfutsa narrated the story to us last summer when we visited with Khriebu?'

'I forgot. Tell me', Vime loved stories and she eagerly snuggled closer to listen better, the tip of her nose almost touching Neime's as she did so.

'It's an old folktale, Vime, about a girl who was mistreated by her stepmother. And so, to escape, she began weaving a cloth with only black and white yarn. This colour combination was quite unusual so visitors would often ask her about it and she would reply that she was weaving a pair of wings for herself. She rightly predicted that in future, when she is gone, young men would adorn themselves with her fine black-and-white feathers. When the day finally came that she finished her weaving, she donned the wings which instantaneously transformed her into a hornbill and flew far away. And so, legend has it that the great hornbill was actually once a girl who just could not bear to be human. But happily, for her, she doesn't remember her past life anymore, forever soaring the skies until human life became nothing but a dim memory. That's what I mean, Vime, when I said we can always fly away', Neime finished with a bright smile but Vime thought her lower lip quavered tellingly.

Vime took a deep breath, satisfied and fascinated with the story's ending, but also thinking of Mother in the in-between. She had a better plan. Was it finally time to tell Neime? Could Neime handle it? She was almost on the verge of testing her sister when Neime turned round her back and abruptly changed the subject. The moment had passed.

'Father gave me some money so that we can buy new dresses. I thought maybe we can go shopping this Saturday.'

'What for?'

Neime's silence was all the answer Vime needed. It really was happening, a pang in the heart told her. Neime didn't mean what she said, she was only telling a story.

'I don't need a new dress. I'll wear the black one Mother made for me. Anyway, I thought there wasn't going to be a wedding ceremony', Vime stated

'Regardless, we still have to dress nicely that day. People will come and pictures will be taken', Neime insisted, thinking herself quite persuasive. 'And you certainly can't wear black that day.'

'Why not? Mother always lets me wear what I want. She wouldn't have had a problem.'

Neime got up and looked down at Vime who was also sitting up now, a stubborn look in her eyes. The tranquil mood had shifted and they now looked at each other, miffed and annoyed.

'Vime, you're not the only one scared, not the only one who misses Mother.'

'Feels like it, sometimes.'

'I'm sorry but I have to say this. You can be very self-absorbed, you know that? What good does it do anyone to wallow in misery? We have to move on, accept what we cannot change.'

'So go ahead and move on, who's stopping you. Just let me be', Vime insisted.

'Mother told me to look after you . . . ', Neime began and it really was the worst thing she could have said.

'I don't need anyone to look after me. I can look after myself just fine!' Vime suddenly shouted, her face flushed, quite visibly upset.

'Who cooks your meals, who cleans . . . ', Neime began hotly and then stopped, suddenly looking very tired. Spoiling for a fight, Vime wished she would just continue.

'Vime, I don't want to fight anymore', Neime said instead and she sounded drained, like she meant it.

'Neither do I', Vime glumly agreed.

'It's late, let's get some sleep and talk tomorrow.'

Neime got up to leave. As she was closing the door behind her, Vime who always wanted the door to her room shut, gripped by instinctive terror all of a sudden, said, 'No, don't close it completely, leave it ajar.'

Neime looked at her oddly but did as she asked. After Neime left, Vime mutely stared up the ceiling, dwelling over the futility of her circumstances—inner demons raging within, overwhelming her with a thick cloud of gloomy despair.

TWELVE

'I told you to stop it!' Vime exclaimed loudly, feeling quite irate with whoever or whatever mischievous being was trailing after her, throwing little stones and gravelly earth from behind the trees and bushes. It came from a different direction each time she turned. Although she did not have the nerve to face Tei in the forest, she couldn't resist a brief little stroll down her favourite cobbled footpath. Vime needed to get away from the house with all its old sad memories and new ones that were soon going to be foisted on her if she did not find a way out. Khrielie would be marrying Father very soon. She seemed nice enough, but Vime grimly contemplated how all stepmothers in her storybooks started out nice and became horrid later. Neime's story had certainly been no better.

Her strategy to avoid meeting Tei was turning back before reaching the rice fields which preceded the forest. But today, the solitary walk, which was supposed to ease her overladen mind, was disrupted by whatever was lurking behind the shadows. The mysterious harassment

began after she had crossed the ancient kharü. Vime had
initially suspected a certain gang of rowdy neighborhood
boys who were known for making nuisances of themselves.
However, she now doubted that they would be so skillful
in evading her.

Just as Vime was about to yell her frustration a second
time, she saw a familiar and altogether welcoming figure
coming towards her from the opposite end of the lane. It
was the same woman she had encountered in the forest
the last time she met Tei. Recognizing Vime, the woman
called out genially:

'Neinuo, I hope you're not playing truant from
school again?'

Feeling fairly sheepish, Vime self-consciously waited
for the woman to come closer but she was saved from
answering because the woman said she was only teasing.

'You must eat a lot of vegetables', Vime remarked,
eyeing the woman's khorü filled with forest greens like the
last time.

The woman's words tinged were with laughter; 'It's not
all for me. I sell vegetables at the market. But these here,
these are for Ani Sebu. She always prefers to buy her greens
from me.'

Vime quite liked her neighbour Mrs Sebu, whose
house was just around the corner. She decided to join
the woman to Mrs Sebu's house. The woman's name was
Ajano and she declined to stay and rest after unloading her
khorü, explaining that her little children would be missing
her at home.

'Poor woman. Her husband is not around and she has
to single-handedly look after all their five children', Mrs

Sebu remarked as she proceeded to arrange the vegetables into their respective baskets in her neat and orderly kitchen.

'Where's her husband?' Vime asked.

'He's a soldier in the Naga Army and so he can't be home with his family', Mrs. Sebu explained. Like most children around her, Vime was familiar with the Naga Army but understood little. She did know that they wanted the Naga Hills to be free of the present Indian government and because of that, couldn't move about freely because they were regarded as insurgents. Her friend Khriebu's uncle had also joined the movement and she often spoke proudly of him. Not interestedly in politics, however, Vime didn't ask further.

'Would you like some kemenya cake?' Mrs Sebu offered, holding up a tray of neatly arranged and uniformed slices of sticky rice cake, much to Vime's delight. Her walk had whipped up an appetite and she just realized that she was famished.

'Yes, very much please, Aunty.' Vime answered enthusiastically, while helping herself to a slice.

Mrs Sebu briskly cleaned a bundle of vegetables, shaking fresh earth off them, while Vime enjoyed a glass of creamy milk with her sweet and chewy treat.

'I hear your father is remarrying soon then? Khrielie, I heard?'

'Yes', Vime answered without looking up, her attention on the little crumbs which had fallen into the milk.

'Is she nice?'

Vime quietly wondered why adults liked to talk about such mundane things. Mrs Sebu seemed disappointed when Vime only nodded without volunteering further information. Feeling that she should make up by saying something interesting, Vime revealed:

'Aunty, do you know what happened today after I crossed the old crumbling village gate?'

'You mean the kharü?'

'Yes', Vime replied and animatedly went to describe how something impish kept throwing little stones at her.

'It first started with a few stray bits of pebbles which soon became clusters of little stones and gravelly sand. I think it was trying to goad me. The angrier I got, the more the throwing increased', Vime perceptively thought aloud as she imagined a sense of glee behind the mischievous activity.

Mrs Sebu promptly advised Vime not to explore the forest or go past the kharü as frequently as she did and especially not alone, 'These forests are very old. And till today, our people fear the kharü for good reason. Many elaborate sacred rituals known as nanyüs, pertaining to our ancestral spiritualism are attached to village gates.'

'Oh, but I'm not scared', Vime replied with nonchalant alacrity.

'Well, you should be', the woman replied firmly, adding that it was wise to have healthy respect for such things. 'Young girls ought not to be too adventurous', the woman remarked, suddenly reminding Vime of Atsa Neidonuo. She would have retorted had it been the latter. But Vime held back as Aunty Sebu was always nice to her and especially because she suddenly imagined mother's embarrassment if she learned that her younger daughter had behaved impertinently towards their pleasant neighbour.

Thoughtfully contemplating Mrs Sebu's words, Vime asked: 'Are some forests really older than others?'

She had first heard this from Ajano, the vegetable vendor, during their meeting in the forest. Vime had not given it much thought then. Not until Mrs Sebu repeated the adjective about the forest.

'Of course. Just like there are old and young people, so also there are old and young forests.'

'And old forests are where spirits reside', Vime concluded helpfully.

Mrs Sebu looked quite taken aback over Vime's calm matter-of-fact statement. What an odd little thing this girl is, the woman thought, studying Vime's clear-cut features; the deep-set brown, almond-shaped eyes and sweet upturned nose set within an oval shaped face framed by hair practically chopped just below the chin and always firmly tucked behind her ears. Observing Vime's slim boyish frame perched by the edge of the sofa, enjoying milk and cake, Mrs Sebu said:

'Now, Vime, I know precious little about forest spirits. But I do know that our world is old. And some people believe that there are still places which spirits call home, where tired souls go to rest after their bodies have grown weary of living. Your uncle, my husband, is from Longkhum, a beautiful little vanguard village situated high above the clouds. Legend has it that Longkhum is a place where tired souls go to rest, manifesting as eagles after death.'

Vime leaned forward eagerly, keen to learn more. The woman grinned, quite pleased with her own story but to Vime's sharp disappointment, she concluded: 'Fascinating legends, aren't they? But of course, they are just that. Myths and legends.'

Seeing Vime's painfully obvious crestfallen expression, Mrs Sebu quickly made amends by whispering confidingly:

'You know, when I was a young girl like you, my mother would unfailingly throw a sprig of ciena plant inside my khorü whenever I was to go to the woods. It was believed to repel malevolent spirits. I wasn't brave like you and used to be petrified of passing the kharü, what with all the extraordinary stories around it. My zealous mother taught me to chant 'Sky Father Earth Mother' and other ancestral prayers for protection whenever I could sense danger. Of course, that was before we all became Christians. It was a different world then, Vime. A more dangerous world, I should say. We were so vulnerable to spiteful spirits and lived in constant fear as a result.'

An engrossed Vime released a happy little shudder, which Mrs Sebu mistook as alarm.

'Ah listen to me, rambling on about old fears. I hope you won't have trouble sleeping tonight.'

'Oh, no, I love these stories, Aunty. Can you tell me more?'

Mrs Sebu laughed, 'Stories go to the bold, Vime, to those who seek it. I was too timid to become a storyteller. Hence, I never had any spirit encounters. You know, since I often had to go to the forest to work our field, the one spirit I dreaded seeing the most was Chükhieo, the guardian spirit of wildlife.'

'So, you never saw him, then?' Vime asked, brown eyes wide and mouth agape. Her own grandfather had spoken of Chükhieo who would protect his animals by confusing hunters, which sometimes led to tragic deaths wherein a hunter would mistake his hunting partner for a wild creature.

'No, I never saw him but my late hunter father did, many times. Father would always say Chükhieo had been good to him whenever he was able to hunt good game.'

Vime laughed appreciatively; she found the idea of a spirit gifting animals to humans quite delightful and somewhat amusing too. She hoped Mrs Sebu would continue and was disappointed when she looked out the open windows instead and said, 'Goodness, I better close the windows before the mosquitoes get in. It's getting dark, enough for today, Neinuo. You should be getting home now.'

Vime got up reluctantly. Mrs Sebu invited her to stay for dinner but Vime politely declined as it seemed an afterthought. Anyway, Mrs Sebu's husband would be returning soon and Vime found the woman's husband too austere to feel comfortable around him. She couldn't imagine spending an entire dinner with him.

'Mind my words about going to the forest alone, won't you?' Mrs Sebu reminded Vime.

Vime nodded. She thanked Mrs Sebu for the refreshment and story, and took her leave after promising to visit again soon.

'Now, go straight home, alright?' Mrs Sebu called out a final time before Vime exited the door.

Her head filled with Aunty Sebu's forest spirits, Vime was about to cross the road when she heard strains of a haunting melody from the forest. Somehow Vime instinctively knew it was Tei's forest song although it sounded completely different this time, not remotely charming or nostalgic like she remembered. It made her feel strange; incomplete, like her insides had grown hollow, soulless. The song itself sounded like a half-remembered melody, like someone playing a song they did not know how to play and that too, coaxed, forced out rather, from rusty old musical instruments which remained un-tuned for too long. The jarring melody made the hairs on Vime's arms and neck prick and stand on end. The unnatural music became increasingly louder until Vime almost believed the sound literally came from inside her head. Her heart thumping violently, Vime covered her ears with her hands and ran home, uncaring that people were staring at her, feeling safe only after she was inside her room, huddled underneath her blankets.

THIRTEEN

Rain drizzled throughout the night before Khrielie's arrival. In the morning, a dense mist had settled, invasively seeping everywhere, in and around the entire town. There was an eerie calm which trickled into the ripe afternoon. Acutely conscious of the unusual lull in the air, Vime looked out of the mist-whitened opaque windows and grimly pronounced that the devouring fog had absorbed all living sounds.

'Really, Vime. You are too young to be so morose! More likely, this freezing weather has driven both man and beast to take shelter. That's why it's so quiet', Grandmother chided as she continued with the muffler she had been knitting since the past hour. Vime's grandparents had arrived from the village to receive Khrielie who would be reaching soon, accompanied by her relatives.

The front doors threw themselves wide open suddenly and mist crawled inside the house. Resisting the absurd urge to literally sweep away the encroaching miasma with a broom, Vime hastily closed the doors, standing on tiptoes upon a stool and firmly twisted the top latch to prevent it from loosening again.

'Vime dear, why are you so edgy? Come here, sit by me and help me unravel this ball of yarn', Grandmother called out. She must have assumed that Vime was nervous about Khrielie as she abruptly began rambling on about what a nice person Khrielie actually is. Poor Atsa, so unaware of how obviously transparent she could be, Vime secretly thought in amusement, enjoying a brief moment of levity. She took a moment to take in the scene around her. Grandmother had nicely seated herself upon Mother's favourite armchair, soft and comfortably worn out with age. Beside Grandmother was the rusty old metal thezhübou, a traditional heater, filled to the brim with red-hot charcoal fire spitting spiritedly. Close by, the cat contentedly lay curled into a sleepy ball atop Grandmother's feet. Neime was helping Ania Ataü with dinner in the kitchen and Vime could hear them talking between bursts of merry laughter. Everyone seemed relaxed and gay. Vime suddenly envied her family's lightheartedness. It made her feel incredibly alone, alienated from everyone, burdened by unspoken fears which she couldn't bring herself to share. She had unwittingly gone in too deep now. Ever since leaving Aunty Sebu's house that evening, Tei's forest song had been visiting her each night, unfailingly turning dreams into nightmares. Each time, the song sounded even more twisted than she remembered. Although Vime had slept, she'd wake up feeling exhausted, like she had stayed awake singing the entire night.

'Atsa, I want to ask you something', Vime said to Grandmother very seriously.

'What is it?'

'Do you think that spirits can manifest through songs in dreams?'

'Why, Vime! Why are you asking this?' her eighty-six-year-old childlike grandmother stopped her knitting and sat up, looking very alarmed suddenly.

'No reason in particular. It's just something Khriebu told me; you know how we enjoy exchanging ghost stories', Vime lied, trying to sound as blasé as possible.

Grandmother expelled a rather exaggerated sigh (or so Vime thought) and answered:

'I don't know. That's a very specific question.' Still looking a little concerned, the elderly woman admonished Vime not to be too taken with the supernatural. It's not healthy, was all the explanation she offered. Vime just wanted the evening to be done with and was glad when Khrielie finally arrived with a few of her relatives. Father had requested the local pastor to come and pray for him and his new wife. A sumptuous dinner followed after the pastor blessed the new couple. Very soon, Khrielie was waving goodbye to her relatives, surrounded by her new family—her husband and his two daughters. Vime's grandparents as well as Ania Ataü all departed the same time as Khrielie's relatives.

'Well, it's getting cold out here, shall we go in?' Father suggested as the newly formed family continued to linger even after the guests were out of sight. Neime was the first to go back inside the house.

'Yes, it's going to be an unusually cold winter this year', Khrielie agreed conversationally. Their guests had been served tea after partaking dinner and seeing Vime gather the empty tea cups strewn around, Khrielie asked, 'So Vime, which delicious item did you prepare tonight?'

Vime's fair skin turned visibly bright red in embarrassment. 'Neime and Ania Ataü cooked everything', she muttered.

Father laughed and explained that Vime had helped in other ways and added that the floral arrangement on the dining table was Vime's work.

'It's beautiful. Thank you, Vime', Khrielie said, feeling a sense of empathetic kinship towards the young girl who looked terribly uncomfortable to be the centre of attention. Vime muttered that she had plucked the flowers from the wayside. She had a bright artificial smile pasted on her expressive face, and once again, Khrielie remembered their brief conversation not too long ago.

That night, Vime took out her journal. She had started writing regularly now. It eased her somehow. There was also a troubling thought which kept niggling at the back of her mind although she tried to repress it—a little voice which told her that her journal would perhaps help her family understand better, if ever anything happened to her.

December 8: Khrielie came home to become father's new wife tonight. Neime seems really happy now. I think Tei is trying to reach out to me. I keep having nightmares of the forest song. I am sure it was Tei who sent the rain and mist today. Grandmother didn't think anything was amiss about today's weather but that's because she doesn't know what I know.

That night, she forced herself to stay awake, rearranging her books, folding and refolding her clothes, then finally staring up the ceiling, trying to wait out the night. Vime wanted to sleep in the comfort of daylight but try as she might, sleep overcame her eventually. And the thing she had been dreading soon began. Vime dreamt that the forest song could be heard in every corner of the house. In her dream, Ania Ataü's face appeared misshapen, bizarrely grotesque as she wailed, 'What have you done? Why have you brought this unearthly music here?' while Father and Neime's blurred and distorted figures hovered in the background. The nightmare jolted her wide awake, wiping every trace of sleep. Vime sat upright on her bed, drenched in sweat, her heart hammering inside her chest like a trapped little animal. The dream felt so real and she strained her ears for any supernatural presence in the room. But all she could hear was the night sound of crickets up high alongside the croaking of frogs, dismal and low baritone.

'Tei? Are you here?' Vime called out, her slight frame stiff and tense, the heavy blanket protectively pulled up till just below her eyes. But the consuming darkness only answered with ominous silence. Vime could not sleep after that. She desperately looked out the window, willing the dawn to hasten and rescue her.

FOURTEEN

Vime wasted no time getting up as the first morning light softly streamed through her windows. As she went downstairs, she was surprised to find Khrielie already up and bustling about the kitchen. It was a frosty morning but the kitchen looked warm and inviting with the fireplace lit, ready to greet the day.

'Good morning. I see I'm not the only early riser in this house!' Khrielie remarked in genuine surprise. She looked bothered when Vime explained that she wasn't but that she had not been able to sleep properly last night.

Vime sat herself beside the fireplace and gratefully accepted the cup of warm milk that Khrielie proffered. As she sipped her milk, she watched Khrielie expertly prepare a galuo dish. Khrielie scooped a generous spoonful of dzacie-fermented soyabean neatly packed inside a bamboo leaf, and stirred the blend into a sturdy cooking pot filled with water on the boil. She then huddled down the floor with the mortar pestle. Generously sprinkling salt over fresh green chilies, Khrielie deftly ground the mixture into a rough paste and scraped the mixture into the pot. What followed was a quick mash of ginger and garlic accompanied with a scoop of dried lard, for flavour. Finally, she added smoked meat and finished with a generous sprinkle of fragrant sun-dried herb, neitso. Soon, the kitchen was filled with the aromatic smell of dzacie, neitso and smoked meat, while a pot of white rice steamed and simmered nearby.

Father soon joined them downstairs, appreciatively sniffing the fragrant aroma which had filled the spacious kitchen while simultaneously telling Khrielie that it wasn't right that she should be up so early, cooking no less, and especially not on her first day of marriage.

'Besides, we still have plenty of leftovers from last night's dinner', Father said, opening the lids and peering inside the pots.

'It's no trouble. I enjoy cooking. It relaxes me', Khrielie answered.

Observing Father being so nice and attentive towards Khrielie, Vime felt quite outraged on Mother's behalf. She thought he had never been half as solicitous towards Mother when she was alive.

Seeing the easy comfortable way Khrielie moved about the house, Vime idly wondered what had transpired between her and Father in the bedroom last night. At school, she had been privy to hushed whispers about what Vime considered the appalling things men and women do together in private. In her innocence, Vime believed that this could only happen in bed and only between married couples. She had also heard some hilarious stories where the most crucial bit of information somehow always seemed shrouded in mystery. She suspected this was because even the gossipers did not fully know themselves. But Vime knew because Mother had prepared her.

One day, not long after Mother got sick, she had asked a restless Vime to sit beside her and listen attentively. Mother went on to explain to Vime how within the next few years or any day now perhaps, she would find herself bleeding. 'Now, no need to be alarmed when this happens. You aren't hurt. This is something every healthy woman goes through and is a sign that your body is now physically preparing to have babies.' Mother then finally revealed the purpose behind the mysterious soft packets which she kept in ample quantities inside a bag in the bathroom. Vime had once made the mistake of asking about it in Neime's presence and had been infuriated by Neime's smugly condescending look as Mother replied, 'I'll explain when you get a little older.'

Mother would often try to bring the sisters closer together by involving them both in whatever conversation or activity she had planned. Nevertheless, instinctively knowing that Neime had already begun menstruating, Vime was glad that Mother had chosen to speak to her alone that day. Once again, she marvelled over how Mother always seemed to know exactly what to do. Vime cherished the memory of that crisp spring afternoon when Mother and she had conversed like two equal adults, discussing what it was like to be women, and on sex and love. But as Mother went on to predict how she and Neime, too, would eventually fall in love and marry one day, for the first time in her life, Vime saw her eternally cheerful Mother lose control and become teary-eyed; almost distressed. It was alarming. It was only then that she realized just how sick Mother really was.

'Don't worry, it's the medicines that's making me so emotional. Be a good girl now and call Neime, will you?' Mother had said, bringing their happy conversation to an end.

Mother was long gone now and she still hadn't started bleeding. Vime anxiously wondered if she should speak to Neime about it. She looked at Khrielie and wondered when it had happened for her. Would she have babies with Father soon? Just then, as if sensing her thoughts, Khrielie turned round and caught Vime studying her intently. Vime flushed a deep crimson and not knowing what to say, looked away and stared into the fire, her clear brown eyes reflecting the flickering flames although all she could see, really, was Tei—mean and bristling with spite, waiting for her in a dark lonely forest.

FIFTEEN

'Father, I'll be careful, I promise. I've already missed too many days of school', Vime pleaded. Despite the ceasefire, there had been another shootout between the Indian Armed Forces and the Naga Army late last night. The aftermath of violent clashes always inevitably created an uneasy atmosphere, thick and heavy with tension and uncertainty. Father had gone to a neighbour's house early in the morning and returned, his face long and grim, darkened with worry. There were already rumours circulating regarding an impending showdown between the two armies. Father didn't think it was wise to attend school today.

As Vime begged to be allowed to attend school, father hemmed and hawed, not sure what to do. After his remarriage, he had been making a conspicuous effort, going the extra mile to please his daughters. Vime knew this, and sometimes, she took perverse pleasure in taking full advantage. And today, she especially needed to go to school as it would give her the perfect opportunity to sneak to the forest later. Her vivid nightmare still lingered and she constantly worried that Tei might come looking for her if she did not visit soon. Vime also wanted to get away from everyone and rein in her thoughts. The walk to school would do the trick.

In desperation, Vime did something she never thought she'd do. She turned to Khrielie who was listening nearby. All Vime did was throw Khrielie a plaintive look and the latter understood.

'Oh, let her go if she really wants to. Vime's a big girl now', Khrielie chimed in.

In the end, Father, unable to withstand united feminine resistance for too long, gave in.

It turned out that school was closed that day on account of last night's shooting. Along with Vime, a few other students had also turned up, and amongst them was Vime's friend Khriebu.

'I wish there was a teacher so we can at least give our attendance', Khriebu complained. She was the most sincere student in class.

'Yes, well, maybe tomorrow we can inform Teacher that we were present today'', Vime consoled her.

'If school reopens tomorrow', Khriebu grumbled.

As always, the disturbance resulted in the streets wearing a familiarly deserted look. Most of the shops were closed and the bold few which had opened in the morning had their shutters halfway down already, getting ready to close. As the two girls walked home together, Khriebu briefed Vime on the many lessons that she had missed. School had not been priority for Vime in the recent past.

'So, you'll probably need to submit an explanation letter to the headmaster from your father . . . you know, explaining the reason for your absence. Otherwise, you may not be allowed to sit for the exams', Khriebu finished ominously, her voice threateningly low with a depth of emotion which made Vime's lips quiver as she swallowed laughter. Missing exams was the absolute worst thing Khriebu could imagine. But Vime was also reminded what a good friend Khriebu was, always so concerned on her behalf.

'Oh, yes, sure, that won't be any problem. I can get Father to do anything these days', Vime carelessly exclaimed, feeling a little mean but it was only Khriebu, she reasoned. Vime paused, and then abruptly stated, 'Father got remarried.'

'Yes, I heard. Congratulations to him, I guess. What is she like? I've only seen her a few times', Khriebu remarked.

'She's alright.'

The two girls continued walking in comfortable silence until they had almost reached the intersection which would separate their routes. Vime presumptuously expected Khriebu to invite her home for tea like she usually did and wondered what explanation she could offer for declining, without giving offence. She wouldn't have worried over such triflings in the past but they were only just renewing their friendship after a prolonged lull. Khriebu with her generous spirit had glossed over Vime's increasingly sullen behaviour during their last few meetings, no questions asked, and Vime didn't want to take her friend for granted this time. She thought of teatime at Khriebu's and how her friend's mother, Apfo Neilaü, always seemed happy to have her, never failing to serve them the most scrumptious snacks along with tea. It suddenly dawned on Vime that she had missed these old comforts but she decided that settling affairs with Tei ought to be priority for now. She soon realized, however, that she needn't have concerned herself over what excuse to offer because for the first time, her friend didn't invite her home. She uncomfortably wondered whether Khriebu was still secretly angry with her for neglecting their friendship for so long.

Perhaps Khriebu sensed this because she went on to explain, 'Listen Vime, I'd like to invite you over for tea. Mother would love that too . . . but . . . today is not a good time . . .'

Embarrassed, Vime quickly interrupted, 'Oh, no, don't explain. I'm always having tea at your place, rather shamelessly. In fact, I want to invite you over. It's been too long. Please come and meet Khrielie too.'

Khriebu's anxious face broke into a radiant grin and she nodded her head enthusiastically, promising to visit very soon. Something that was believed irreversible fixed itself just then, and suddenly, the two girls found themselves being silly, giggling uncontrollably over nothing, being carefree schoolgirls, just like old times. It made Vime feel a lot more like her old self.

Khriebu hugged Vime and burst out, 'Listen Vime, I have to tell you a secret. But first, you have to promise me you won't say a word to anyone.'

'A secret?! Yes, of course, I promise', Vime promptly stuck out her little finger for a pinky swear.

After sealing the promise, Khriebu asked,

'Remember my Uncle Zhabu? My mother's younger brother?'

'The one who went underground?'

'No Vime, don't call them "underground". They are national workers, fighting for our rights as a free people. But yes, him. He's a secret guest at home right now so Mother says we have to be careful and avoid having visitors. I'm only telling you because you are my best friend.'

'Don't worry, my lips are sealed. Who will I tell? Neime?' Vime rolled her eyes sarcastically and Khriebu laughed. 'Why is he visiting secretly?' Vime asked.

'Because he is wanted by the Indian Army. And Mother and I will also be in trouble for harbouring him. Vime, there's so much happening around us in our own lands with our people that we are not learning in schools. I will tell you everything after Uncle leaves, I promise.'

Taken aback, Vime solemnly promised. She almost felt tempted to share her own secrets as well and she might have but Khriebu seemed anxious to get home. Just as well, Vime thought.

'You mustn't breathe a word of this to anyone', Khriebu emphatically admonished a final time before biding Vime the last of quite a few goodbyes while standing on the crossroads.

Vime noticed a few excited neighbourhood kids snooping behind a tree near her house. As she drew closer, she instantly understood why, as she spied three tall men in camouflaged uniform outside the compound jointly shared by a few houses including hers. Time and again, the Indian Army would conduct 'surprise checking' on residential houses. This was a scene Vime had witnessed many times but it still made her nervous, although Father had said there was no reason to be since they had not done anything wrong. She had wanted to sneak inside her heavy school bag at home and if possible, change clothes before leaving for the forest but seeing the soldiers, Vime decided to head directly to the forest.

Vime had an instinctive sense that her dreams were threatening to spill into the waking hours. She did not have a clear-cut plan yet but delaying seemed a worse idea. She needed to meet Tei and pacify her before things got out of hand. Knowledge of the in-between had been a comfort to Vime ever since she had discovered its existence. Now, every time she missed Mother, she reminded herself that all was not lost and this made her yearn for Mother more than ever before. Vime was convinced that Tei was lonely although her snooty nature would never allow her to admit it. Perhaps, I can persuade her to help me meet Mother if only for one brief moment, in exchange for regular visits from me (which she'd have to offer most tactfully, lest Tei reacts scornfully).

SIXTEEN

As Vime neared the crossroads, she heard strains of the forest song, melodious and faintly haunting, beckoning her like a siren call. As she listened, something inexplicably strange stirred within, making her heart lurch. Her skin prickled sensitively while painful memories suddenly flooded her mind like a fever pitch. Just then, as she helplessly proceeded to respond to the evocative call of the song in a trance-like manner, her foot painfully struck an innocuous little stone lying on her path. Shaken out of her reverie and slightly annoyed thus, Vime looked down to see a faded hopscotch diagram scratched upon the asphalt covered road. She picked up the culprit of a stone and inspected it with the expert eyes of a seasoned hopscotch player. Somebody had carelessly forgotten a lucky stone, she thought. It was quite perfect for the game, nicely flat and solid. Vime threw down her bag, crouched a little and lightly flung the stone. It landed on the desired square with a satisfying thud. On one foot, she hopped through the squares, skipping the one with the stone, turned, retrieved the stone and hopped back to the beginning home square.

'Excellent!', Vime thought, cradling the stone with visible delight, unconsciously smiling to herself. Khriebu and she were both hopscotch enthusiasts and while she grudgingly acknowledged that her best friend might possibly be the more skillful player of them two, Vime felt fairly certain that possessing a lucky stone was half the game won. Surely this stone would give her the winning edge henceforth, she thought gleefully. Just then, a huge green Indian Army truck with its familiar camouflaged safety nets all around the back lumbered up the hill. Quickly and nervously, Vime dropped the stone inside her pocket, picked up her school bag and cleared the road, trying to make herself as inconspicuous as possible by blending into the surrounding foliage lining the pavement. She wondered whether the soldiers had finished 'checking' her house. Sometimes they were polite and made small talk with Father but often, they would unceremoniously turn the entire house upside down, which would invariably upset her late mother, who kept a neat house, and make her go tight-lipped. But no one ever said anything to protest, not Father nor Mother. Nor did she or Neime ever ask why. Despite Vime's youthful innocence, and although she didn't completely understand, an instinctive wisdom warned that some indignities were best left alone.

Suddenly Khriebu's uncle came to mind. Oh no, I must warn them! Vime thought in alarm, feeling incredibly guilty that she had not thought of her best friend sooner. Feeling like the worst of friend, Vime sprinted below the road, taking a shortcut by cutting across the woods. It was only later that she would wonder with a chill as to why the forest song had not sung in that brief expanse of wooded area she passed through.

From down below, Vime ascended uphill and finally emerged upon a low flattened hilltop overlooking Khriebu's house. Often, when she didn't feel like going inside the house or meeting any adults, she would call out to Khriebu from her vantage position which faced Khriebu's room window. This hilltop was one of their many secret hideouts.

'Khriebu, Khriebu!', Vime called out frantically, out of breath, her voice slightly high-pitched and shrill from nervousness. The back door opened quickly, as if Vime was expected. This time, however, it wasn't Khriebu but her mother Apfo Neilaü who responded. There was no welcoming smile on her face this afternoon. Instead, she looked immensely grim and gestured for Vime to come down and inside the house. As Vime obediently scrambled down, she could see Khriebu standing behind her mother, her face screwed into a frowny expression which Vime knew wordlessly conveyed what-are-you-doing-didn't-I-tell-you?

Without any preliminaries, Apfo Neilaü put a stiff arm around Vime and said, 'Khriebu, why don't you take Vime to your room?'

'No, Apfo Neilaü, I can't stay. I just came to tell you that the Army is conducting house-to-house checking at this very moment. They were at my house when I reached home and they'll be here soon. I took a short cut. I just came to warn you', Vime finished hurriedly.

Apfo Neilaü looked at her and then at Khriebu as comprehension dawned. She hurried back inside the house and Vime could hear shuffling noises and people talking in low tones. Khriebu and Vime looked at each other anxiously.

'Thank you, Vime', Khriebu said, her face lit with a tremulous little smile, still looking understandably anxious.

'I hope you won't get into trouble for telling me.'

'Oh, no, no, not at all! I'm glad I told you', Khriebu assured her.

'Oh, good. Well, I better get going. No, don't bother', Vime said as Khriebu turned to tell her mother that Vime was leaving.

The two girls hugged quickly.

'I hope your uncle will be safe', Vime said. As she paused to adjust the strap of her school bag uncomfortably weighing down her right shoulder, she felt the stone press against her skin. Vime impulsively extracted the little stone from inside her pocket and very deliberately, carefully placed it inside the palm of Khriebu's right hand. Her friend looked understandably puzzled as she did so, looking at the stone and then at her, waiting for an explanation.

'Take it. I'm pretty certain it'll bring luck. I'll explain another time, I promise', Vime whispered before taking off finally.

When she looked back down from the hilltop for a final glance, Vime saw three men standing alongside Apfo Neilaü and Khriebu. They were all uniformly dressed in green but looked somewhat unkempt, not as smartly dressed as the other party. Two of them stood a little further apart and waited while the third enfolded Khriebu and her mother together in his arms and appeared to be talking to them rather affectionately. That must be Khriebu's uncle, Vime surmised. After the three broke apart, as if feeling Vime's keen stare, Khriebu's uncle looked up and stared straight at Vime, a hand up to cover his eyes from the sun's blinding white glare.

Quite uncharacteristically, quiet and reserved Vime gave a little wave which Khriebu's uncle returned uncertainly with his free hand. Satisfied that she had completed her mission, Vime turned and left.

Her head abuzz with fanciful romantic theories about Khriebu's uncle, Vime almost forgot to take the turn towards the forest. As she pondered over the forest song and how it had abruptly ended and sang no more while she crossed the woods on her way to warn Khriebu earlier, a perceptive Vime began to comprehend the limited reach of Tei's forest song. She recalled how the spirit had once told her that she had been out of reach during the happier past as she had been too absorbed with life. No wonder Ajano, the cheerful vegetable seller, had never seen Tei although she was a regular in the forest. I guess the happiest are immune to Tei and her forest song, Vime resignedly concluded with a heavy sigh. There was a small part of her, burgeoning, growing stronger each passing day, which did not want to part from this world and her life so soon. It protested with little aches in the heart whenever Vime imagined how she would convey her final goodbyes to loved ones in secret or never having to experience life's little pleasures again. Vime determinedly squelched this new awareness with a shake of her head, refusing to allow herself to linger on this uncomfortable new feeling. It was too late and anyway, the old sadness was always relentless, she reasoned.

Soon, Vime found herself once more down the cobbled footpath. Something felt strangely odd today, however; there was no spring in her steps as she walked down her favourite place in the whole world. For the first time in her life, Vime sadly realized that it was no longer a place of refuge. Instead, she experienced a sense of trepidation which heightened with every step she took. Vime took a deep breath and willed herself to be brave.

SEVENTEEN

'What do you mean you don't want to be a part of my song?' Tei snarled softly, underlying menace contained within the deceptive softness of her voice.

Vime took a step back as Tei sinuously leaned closer without moving her feet. She had said many other things but Tei had latched on to the one topic of discussion that Vime had wanted to avoid and so had briefly touched upon, only for Tei to interrupt her right then.

'Vime, do you know what it means to break a pact with a spirit?' Tei hissed, alarmingly animal-like. Although her growled words were almost inarticulate, Vime understood well, the veiled threat contained in the tone. There was a hushed silence which weighed heavy over the forest. Vime was convinced that the entire forest was intently listening to their every word, reading even into the silences that weighed in between.

She swallowed nervously before answering:

'Tei, as Kijübode here as my witness, I have not made any promises to break. You've misunderstood. But like I said, I still want to go to the in-between. Can't we work out another arrangement? What would you like?'

Tei's face contorted in malicious rage and Vime thought she looked ready to erupt. But just then, something unpredictably odd happened instead, and Vime wasn't sure whether to be relieved or even more scared. Tei's fiery expression underwent a radical transformation, rapidly changing from fury into barely concealed glee, as if something wonderful had been revealed to her. Bewildered, Vime glanced around their surroundings but all she could see was the grave silence of trees.

Tei's pixie face glowed with anticipation as her thin red lips widened into what might pass for a smile, 'Indeed, you will be coming with me, my dear Vime. But you will not be the only one.'

Gasping aloud, Vime instinctively winced as Tei made a rapid blink-and-you-miss lunging movement towards her. Vime felt a sudden gust of wind hit her but nothing happened. She opened her eyes to find no sign of Tei.

Although Tei was physically gone, the essence of her lingered in the atmosphere as the wind appeared to echo her rather troubling promise. Vime thought the whistling wind was most unnatural because the surrounding foliage and leaves upon the trees remained motionless despite the wind noisily swirling all around.

'What did she mean when she said I would not be the only one?' Vime anxiously pondered, feeling incredibly helpless.

Vime finally accepted that things had gone far beyond her control now (they never really were) and decided to go home and confess everything to Father. He would know what to do. At that moment, Vime felt her young age intensely. I must reach home before Tei returns, Vime thought urgently. But as she turned to leave, she could not find the footpath. It had clean disappeared, just like the day when she first met Tei. As Vime frantically searched in vain, she heard a familiar voice calling her name repeatedly. It was Khrielie, her stepmother. She couldn't make out the direction but Khrielie sounded close by.

'Vime, Vime, where are you?' Khrielie called out, her voice crisp and clear as daylight.

'Hau! Khrielie, I'm here', Vime answered as loudly as she could. But although she had shouted, her voice sounded incredibly muffled even to her own ears. By now, Vime understood how Tei could manipulate the wind to her advantage. This time, it appeared that the supernatural wind was swallowing her voice. The air seemed strangely alive, buzzing with energy and there was an unusual amount of static in the air. Despite what she knew, each time Vime heard Khrielie call her name, she still despairingly tried to answer. As Vime tried to locate the direction of Khrielie's voice, the air slowly swelled into a song which vibrated and hummed in the wind. Vime's heart sank as the forest song filled every corner, drowning all other sounds.

'Khrielie, I'm right here, come to me', Vime heard herself answer. It was her and yet, it wasn't from her. It was the strangest sensation. Vime turned round in circles, involuntarily making herself feel dizzy but still looking around her in utter befuddlement.

'Khrielie, I'm here. Come fast!' Vime heard her own agitated voice call out from outside her body and it sent shockwaves through her.

'I'm coming, stay where you are', Khrielie shouted. The wind had scattered the voices and Vime couldn't make out the direction of sound. But she heard hurried footsteps followed by frantic rustling sounds behind the bushes, as if a small animal had been caught in a trap. Just as suddenly, Khrielie's terrified scream rang clear into the forest, sending birds fluttering high up the air. There was only silence after. Vime felt her insides grow cold and heavy as she instantly understood. Tei had found Khrielie.

No longer searching for the elusive footpath, a petrified Vime blindly entered the thickness of the woods, uncaring as twigs and boughs mercilessly scratched her face and limbs. She trudged onwards, battling brambly scrubs, nettles and the unwelcoming marshy forest floor until she was so exhausted, she helplessly slumped against the trunk of a willowy tree. Everything around her appeared vaguely strange and indistinct. Despite the denseness of the forest, somehow, she could still make out distant fields but they were like the mirages she had read about. The only familiar sight was the tree Kijübode in the place where the earth was birthed. Her vision had blurred and all else appeared hazy except for the tree; for the first time, Vime understood that the tree was the centre of everything. As Vime gazed at the tree, awestruck, she had a primal sense that the tree was staring back at her. Driven by raw instinct, Vime dragged herself up and staggered back to the place where it had all begun.

When she finally reached the foot of the tree, Vime felt utterly drained of energy. She noticed that her bare arms and legs were scratched badly, laced with thin angry red lashes. Bolstered by adrenaline, however, she did not feel any pain. She looked up the tree and squinted as dazzling

light streamed down from above. It made her feel light-
headed and an achingly languid somnolence overcame her
slender body. She felt herself crumple in a slow heavy heap
on the forest floor.

EIGHTEEN

Vime imagined she was dreaming because the tree had a craggy face: bark and sap recalibrating to form a pair of wise weathered eyes, a strong crooked nose and a fine straight mouth. And this rather magnificent visage was looking straight down at her. She thought that the name Kijübode suited the tree very well. It looked noble and extremely old. The word 'primordial' came to Vime's mind. As she continued gazing at the tree in open-mouthed wonder, she noticed that all forms of strange birds and astonishing creatures could be seen perched upon its branches. They were all looking at her, too. Vime wondered whether they had always been there.

'Am I dreaming?' Vime spoke her wonder aloud without meaning to.

'You are in my dream', said the tree. This confused Vime but she didn't ask further. The tree's voice was splendidly deep and sounded ancient and grand, like a wizened old man. Vime instinctively felt a sense of awe and addressed the tree respectfully instead of directly addressing the tree by name.

'Grandfather Kijübode', Vime began haltingly. She must have said the right thing because Vime swore the partly-falcon-partly-prehistoric-like bird perched closest to the tree's face nodded approvingly. Emboldened, Vime continued:

'Can you please help me find Khrielie. I think Tei has her.'

'Young Vime, Tei has indeed captured Khrielie's body. She means to lure you. You must understand this before you set out to rescue Khrielie.'

The tree calmly looked on as Vime unconsciously wrung her hands together, distress mingled with bewilderment. Taking pity on her, Kijübode explained without being asked:

'Think, Vime. Look back. Tei has tricked you into offering yourself to her forest song. Words once spoken, released into the world, remain. After all, this human world began with the Supreme Creator Ukenuopfü's word. Your words are now alive, breathing new strength into her song each time the wind caresses it back and forth. It has made you more vulnerable to her reach, too. Has she not visited you in dreams and songs since your last meeting? She has managed to trap a fragment of you. That was how she could lure and capture Khrielie with your own voice.'

Everything she had been experiencing came back and it all made sense now, 'Why does she want me anyway?'

'It could be anyone, Vime. Know that you are not the first human Tei has tricked. Nor will you be the last. But take heart that she only has a sliver of you. For now. The offer of self to the forest song must come voluntarily from the human. Free will is paramount. Tei has no power to forcibly take as she pleases. That is why she is determined to finish what has begun. Perhaps that is why she has taken Khrielie. Or perhaps she wants you both. More and more human voices to add terrible beauty and vitality to her song.'

Vime felt utterly miserable, 'Grandfather Kijübode, please help me. Tell me what to do.'

'What do you want to do, young Vime?'

'I want to save Khrielie and myself too', Vime replied.

'And your mother? That was what led you here. If I help you, will you give up searching for her?'

Vime was torn. A part of her wanted to say that all she wanted now was to rescue Khrielie. After all, she was responsible. But she could not bear to forego the chance to see Mother again. She found herself helplessly giving in to her heart's anguished yearning.

'Please, Grandfather Kijübode, I want to go through the portal so that I can see Apfo again. Just to see her face one last time', Vime squeaked timidly, looking downwards, shame-faced and not daring to face the tree. She had to ask. She couldn't bear not to.

Although Kijübode remained silent, Vime could feel the tree's as well as many other pairs and single eyes upon her. Finally, when she could bear the silence no longer, Vime looked up. Although she was unaware, her expressive brown eyes reflected a turbulent sea of unexpressed pain and yearning.

Kijübode's gaze was so intense that Vime felt incredibly vulnerable; naked and defenceless. It was as if he was looking into her soul and judging her. She imagined that he must be condemning her for being so weak. The tree's wrinkled face became even more so as he frowned. After a weighed silence, Kijübode's baritone voice boomed.

'Continue to walk down the cobbled footpath and you will find your mother as you remember her.'

If Vime found the tree's words puzzling, she did not get the chance to inquire further because the tree's face realigned, merging into plain crusty bark as did with all the birds and creatures perched upon him.

Meanwhile, the missing footpath had reappeared. As far as Vime knew, the crumbling path ended around the bend. To her surprise, she saw for the first time that the dilapidated trail continued past the tree into the deeper ends of the woods. How had she missed this? But nothing surprised her anymore really. Lying untrodden for so long, stretches of the footpath lay hidden, covered by moss, dead leaves and earth. Vime obediently followed the path, all the while feeling that she was being watched. But it was a comforting sensation, like slowly falling to sleep with the calming knowledge that one was being watched over by a protective parent. The path soon turned into ascending stairs and Vime climbed on until she exited the forest and entered a busy human-inhabited area. There were children noisily playing a game of football in the middle of the road, clearing out and resuming the game in between sporadic traffic.

'Why, this is the area below my house!' Vime exclaimed as realization dawned. Everything appeared the same and yet, different somehow. She felt different too. Vime felt slightly discombobulated, like she was in a dream. Although it was a sunny afternoon, a cover of fog hazed over the entire town, making everything appear surreal and indistinct. Everyone she passed looked right through her as if she didn't exist. At the junction, before reaching her house, Vime saw something she knew wasn't there the last time she passed by (which had only been earlier this afternoon while hugging Khriebu goodbye, Vime marvelled in amazement as it felt a long time ago). It was a splendid bronzed statue of a tall and wirily-built man beside a flag pole. Vime thought there was something incredibly enigmatic about the figure alongside the blue flag with stars and a rainbow, boldly fluttering in the wind.

Vime turned twice to look at the odd fixture but then brushed it off her mind as she determinedly headed home. The door was ajar as always. She gingerly stepped foot inside the house, her heart pounding, hope intermingled with fear, in wary anticipation of what awaited her. Her vision clouded as the fog grew even thicker. The fog appeared to be guiding her as it cleared the path towards the kitchen while all else around her blurred. Vime obeyed the unspoken urging to follow the cleared path. As she entered the familiar kitchen, she could see a familiar silhouette, seated upon a moora and slightly hunched over the fireplace. Mother was humming a tune while stirring a simmering pot.

'Apfo!' Vime cried out, her chest tightly constricted with emotion as she ran towards her mother. But like everyone she had met, she could neither touch nor talk to Mother. Her arms and entire being went through Mother just like the haze around them. Even the objects in the room felt oddly transient. For a brief moment, Vime debated whether she had understood things in reverse and that perhaps she was the one who passed on. Vime cried and shouted, doing just about everything she could to capture Mother's attention. She felt like she was inside an imperceptible bubble, immersed but separate from her surroundings. When Vime, after a great deal of effort, managed to knock down a chair, Mother actually stopped what she was doing and looked around her in confusion. Vime held her breath. Apparently seeing nothing, however, Mother resumed her mundane activities. Finally, Vime gave up. Resigned, she knelt next to Mother and stared at the illusion of the beloved face she had ached to see for so long.

As the sun began to set, Mother got up to close the windows and turn on the night lights. A light fixture behind Vime suddenly flickered and waned, and this caught Mother's attention. As Vime looked into Mother's eyes, she swore her Mother could sense her presence. Mother had a curious expression on her face and a bemused smile played on the corners of her mouth. The mist reappeared and the room, with Mother in it, became grainy and visually indistinct, slowly fading before her eyes. Vime gave a final attempt to hold mother but she was gone.

Although she now understood that the Mother she saw was a chimera, Vime still wept because it reminded her of all that she had lost. She allowed the fog to swirl and dance around her while a heavy listlessness crept into her limbs. Gravity appeared non-existent as she allowed herself to lean against the strength of the vapour. Once again, Vime wondered whether she was in a dream before finally closing her fatigued and heavy eyelids. She woke to Grandfather Kijübode and the strange creatures peering at her.

Vime felt immensely drained, both physically and emotionally, and it made her bolder:

'Grandfather, why can't I talk to Apfo? Why can't she see me?'

Vime heard the tree's voice inside her head, 'You don't need me to tell you why, young Vime. You know the answer to that.'

'Because I'm alive and she's dead', Vime's blunt words tumbled clumsily. She was just so tired.

'On the contrary, your mother has never been more alive. Her soul has been liberated from her decaying body after all.'

'But what did I see, then? Because I saw Apfo! She was in the field Tei took me to, and inside our kitchen just moments ago. Tei said I'm not allowed to approach Apfo because I'm only a visitor.'

'What you saw both times were simply filaments of your own memory. Tei was trying to trap you. You might have discovered the truth had she allowed you to approach the mother you believed you saw.'

'But.. . but.. . how did that happen? How did my memories of Apfo manifest in these strange places? It's not just Apfo or the other human figures that couldn't see me. The place I went appeared just like home except that it wasn't. It had a life-size statue beside a flag which I know for a fact does not exist in the world I know.'

Kijübode appeared intrigued by Vime's revelation. He replied, 'Ah yes, that flag! Such similar sights have infiltrated other realms too. It is the result of a powerful dream which sparked a movement, and in the process, has changed the course of too many lives. The movement still continues to this day and thus, remembrances of it in the realms oscillate between what was and what might be.'

'I don't understand anything anymore', Vime exclaimed unhappily.

Kijübode looked at her sadly, 'I know you don't. Sit down and make yourself comfortable, young Vime. Listen carefully. For you will not hear this story again.'

As Kijübode took a deep breath to become a storyteller once more, all the creatures in the forest gathered around Vime and Kijübode. It had been a long, long time and they wanted to listen to the story again.

NINETEEN

Kijübode's richly timbred voice sounded velvety smooth and sonorous as he began:

In the beginning, the Creator Kepenuopfü created the heavens and the earth.

In those days, the hills too were young and restless, and the spirit and human worlds often merged. Spirits intermingled, warred and married with humankind. But humans were deeply flawed—their greed was endless and they were slaves to emotion. It became impossible to live with such creatures.

And so, the great exodus began. Those proud Kamvüpfis, the demon warriors, were amongst the first to leave, along with great hosts of spirit kinds. They could no longer bear to see the hills, their younger brothers, blown into smithereens and flattened to make roads for man's unnatural machines on wheels. They were soon followed by Miawenuos, those shy spirits who had sadly realized that man only wanted their gifts of riches. The last to leave were Vitsho and Keshüdi, the gatekeepers of hell, who were often seen wandering the deepest forests, their necks crawling with gargantuan worms and maggots. They waited a long time to leave because they wanted their children, the hills and the trees, to come with them. But their long wait was in vain. The hills and trees had been closest to mankind, caring for the human race since the very beginning. They could not bear to leave. And so, they stayed behind, aligning themselves with humans, and in doing so, became keepers of the forests and in time, turned portals between the two worlds, for they were often visited by their spirit kin. I am one of the last surviving of the first trees.

Thus, the two worlds could not remain truly separate. There were also children of spirit and man, the Nephilim. Some were great warriors of old but many became misfits in both worlds. These half human–half spirits kept flitting between the two worlds, creating new spirits of their own. Tei is one such infantile spirit—a mischievous wind spirit known as Zephyr in certain parts of the earth.

It was not easy. The departure of spirits came with grief untold. Many families, lovers, friends, belonging to different natures, man and spirit, were torn apart. Unlike spirits, who are cold-hearted by nature, man's anguish over the loss of a beloved to the spirit world was devastating. For some, their grief proved unrelenting and only grew stronger with time. It breathed life into dormant memories. It was then that the old proud spirits discovered their own fatal imperfection. Mortals, whom they had long scoffed at, were capable of something infinitely precious which was beyond them. Spirits could not love, hence, could not grieve. With this realization, spirits came to envy and covet mortals.

Man's grief proved transcendental. Unbeknownst, it created temporal dimensions in nooks and crevices between the human and spirit world. Fragments of memories of the beloved spirit dwell in these places. Their spirit kin, for love of whom these remembrances formed, took pride in these monuments of love and nurtured them into ephemeral universes. Although transient in nature, many of these dimensions endured even after the passing of their mortal creators. The old immortals for whom these dimensions were unwittingly created, allowed it. Time means nothing to them and they take pride in the very existence of these realms. But with the death of the human creators, the realms began to weaken. The old spirits decided that fresh memories were required to sustain the realms. Memories were added, reshaped and in time, memories of humans interweaved with that of spirits. This is how your own grief-stricken remembrances came to nestle in the realms, being as powerful as they were.

These places are not meant to exist, let alone be visited by the living, even if one has contributed to its continued existence. Often however, a mischievous spirit can lure vulnerable grieving humans into these places.

There was a hushed somber silence when Kijübode finished the telling. Vime remained speechless as she took in all she had heard. Kijübode paused, giving time to let the story sink. When he spoke again, his voice sounded incredibly weary and most humanlike. This time, he addressed Vime directly:

'Vimenuo, you are young and I am old. I have known humans a long time now; certainly, long enough to know that the human experience contains both beauty and terror. Indeed, one cannot exist without the other. And so it is that the Creator Kepenuopfü has designed a time for each under heaven.

Love is Kepenuopfü's greatest gift to man. Spirits envy humans because they cannot love. And certainly, grief is a beautiful child of love undying, borne out of love after all. And yet sometimes, when human sorrow is unyielding, it consumes all else that is still good. When that happens, the sacred circle of joy and sorrow is broken. And it opens the floodgate for all that is cruel and destructive.

Unrelenting bereavement is traitorous and easily exploited by mischievous spirits. Know that only those who yearn for what cannot be found in the living world and have forgone all joys in life can enter the realms. The lure of the memory realms has led many to waste away.'

Vime silently ruminated. The implication that she had no joy in life was as disconcerting as it was sobering.

'Please, Grandfather, I am beginning to understand now. I know I have behaved recklessly but I have realized that I've not lost all love for life.'

'Precisely. And that is why you must now be braver than you have ever been.'

Feeling a fresh surge of courage fuelled by truth, Vime got up her feet. 'Grandfather, help me undo what I've done.'

'I am trying to help you, Vime. That is why I have redirected Tei on her way back here to get you.'

'Where is she? Is Khrielie with her?'

'Tei has hidden Khrielie in one of the in-between spaces, one of her many playgrounds, I know not where. As for Tei herself, I have sent her to a faraway place in this human world where there are oceans and deserts.'

'When will Tei be back? How long do I have?' Vime asked.

'She is already on her way back, I fear. She is cleverer than I expected. You have just enough time to escape the forest. Her hold on you will grow stronger each day, and staying hidden from the forest will no longer shield you but it will give you some time.'

'I can't leave without Khrielie', Vime protested.

Suddenly, sensing a disturbance in the air, the fantastical falcon-like bird perched upon Grandfather Kijübode frantically fluttered and flapped his wings, sending glorious fiery plumes into the air.

The faint notes of the now dreaded forest song whistled in the wind. And yet, Vime knew she couldn't leave without Khrielie.

'Grandfather, please do something to stop Tei!' Vime cried.

Kijübode's grave voice sounded resigned as he spoke, 'It is not in my power, Vime. After all, I am only a tree.'

Vime took a deep breath to steady her nerves and went closer to the tree. Not trusting the wind, Vime cupped her hands around her mouth and softly whispered where she imagined Grandfather Kijübode's ears would be. 'Grandfather, please open the portal. I am going around you now to search for Khrielie. Whatever happens, thank you! I am grateful.'

TWENTY

As Vime scampered around the tree, she heard Grandfather Kijübode give a final warning, 'Young Vime, under no circumstance must you eat anything there'. Before she could react, the earth gave way from beneath her feet.

A deluge of rain welcomed Vime on the other side, forcing her to take cover under a tree. As Vime waited for the rain to subside, she hopefully searched the sheltering tree for traces of a face but found none, much to her disappointment. 'Looks ordinary enough', she concluded with a sigh. The thought of ordinary mundane things filled her with homesickness. She wondered what Father and Neime were doing now and whether she would ever see them again. Vime pressed herself against a cavity hollow around the foot of the tree, trying to make herself as inconspicuous as possible, praying that Tei wouldn't find her. She fervently hoped that Kijübode would give her as much time as possible. When the torrent of rain gradually

gave way, Vime scrambled out the tree and into a little trail
cutting across a flowering mustard field.

A young couple was passing through. The woman
carried a khorü against her back while her husband cradled
a precocious toddler. The mischievous child kept wriggling,
trying to reach for the father's dao dangling inside a wooden
scabbard secured around his waist with a sash. The parents
exchanged fond grins as their child continued his spirited
attempts in vain. They appeared completely oblivious to
Vime's presence although she was standing in plain view.
As they came closer, a startled Vime discovered that that
they were not completely solid. Rather, they appeared
diaphanous. As she watched the blissfully happy family pass
by and fade into the golden hue of blossoming mustard,
Vime wondered whose memory she was in. She looked
around. Beyond were paddy fields and she could see wispy
human figures working on the fields. Just like Mother, none
of these living memories could see or hear her.

Not knowing where Tei might be, Vime dared not call
Khrielie's name out loud. Instead, she began searching for
Khrielie quite indiscriminately in all possible hiding spots,
not unlike playing a game of hide-and-seek, albeit with far
greater stakes at risk. The place was modest in size, consisting
of the mustard field and a few terraced paddy fields. There
was a lonely dahou, the traditional meeting place of the
menfolk, quite isolated and abandoned, at the far edge
where the ground was slightly elevated. As Vime crossed
the dahou, she swore she could hear a thehou, a meeting
of elders, in progress. The circularly arranged sitting places
made of stones were unoccupied and yet deep murmurs
emanated from each stone. Feeling a cold shiver run down

her spine, Vime quickly walked past the dahou until she reached what appeared to be the borderline. A gloomy forbidding darkness bordered the edges of this superficially innocuous place. After searching everywhere, Vime was finally exhausted, and helpless frustration threatened to overcome her. Although she had not yet outgrown a childish fear of the dark, she resolved to be brave and try searching beyond the fields, crossing into the border.

As Vime approached the lurking shadows, she could smell an unpleasant damp mustiness emit from the surrounding black void. And as she drew closer, a waft of something nasty, not unlike rotten eggs, hit her. Undeterred, Vime pinched her nose with her fingers and entered the darkness. She tried to grope her way around as she could see nothing. But within seconds, Vime was soon left gasping for breath and was compelled to turn around. Back on the realm, choking and gratefully inhaling clean air with long-drawn gasps, Vime helplessly knelt on the grass bordering the darkness. She looked around her, the dahou and surrounding fields, and then looked back into the darkness, mystified. This place appeared to exist right in the middle of pitch-blackness filled with thick atmospheric gases. Vime had begun her search with hopeful optimism, daring to believe that of all the many realms, Grandfather Kijübode had purposely chosen to send her here, to this specific place, for a reason. It could not be a random location, she thought. But now Vime could not understand why. She decided to return to the spot where she had taken refuge earlier. As she wearily made her way back, Vime's stomach churned and she realized she was famished. She longingly looked at the mustard plants which enticingly swayed towards her, brushing against her hands as she passed through. But remembering Kijübode's warning, Vime resisted the urge to eat the tender looking greens. Instead, she tightened the arms of her jacket around her waist to quieten her rumbling stomach.

As she drew closer, Vime was surprised to see the same man who had earlier passed by with his wife and son. He was alone this time. He seemed to be looking directly at her. Puzzled, Vime instinctively looked over her shoulders, wondering what he was looking at. He waved then.

Can he see me? Vime first thought to herself and then asked aloud, hopefully, uncertainly; 'Can you see me?' Was he a visitor too like her? But why does he look frail and wispy like the rest of the memories? Vime argued with herself inwardly.

'I've been waiting for you. I wondered where you went', he said.

'Who are you? Are you alive like me?' Vime blurted. She realized how rude her question was if he was not and so she quickly amended by clarifying, 'I don't mean to be impolite. You look like a memory so I'm curious as to how you can see me.'

'I was once called Hevüsa, but am now a living memory, created and unintentionally contained here by my grieving wife who is back in living world. I don't know how I can see you. Perhaps it's because I am half spirit. I am a tekhumiavi.'

Vime's grandfather had told her many tales of tekhumiavis. They were people who had the ability of transforming their spirits into tigers. But this was the first time Vime was meeting one.

Hevüsa was under the impression that Vime had come to visit him and seemed disappointed when he realized that Vime had no knowledge of him. Regardless, when Vime told Hevüsa about Khrielie and how she had been kidnapped by Tei, Hevüsa's tiger spirit revealed itself with a snarl and responded:

'I've never seen Khrielie or any visitor here other than you. But I know of Tei, this mischievous spirit. She has been trying to entrap my wife by enticing her with the forest song for some time now. The old spirits will do naught to stop Tei.'

'The old spirits? You mean the ones for whom these realms were first created?' Vime asked excitedly. 'Where are they? Maybe they can help me.'

'I doubt it. They are watching us even now. But it is beneath them to meddle in affairs concerning humans and lesser spirits. All they care about is the existence of these dimensions. They will not bother to intervene unless anyone or anything threatens or compromises the sanctity of these places.'

Vime tried to calm the rising panic within. She thought of Tei and tried to recall everything she had learned about Tei which might prove useful. She knew she could not afford to waste time by continuing to blindly search for Khrielie until Tei finally arrives.

'Alright, let me go back to the very beginning', Vime exclaimed to herself out loud, agitatedly pacing up and down the floor, like she was wont to whenever in deep concentration. She recalled the place Tei had taken her to first. But that place was intermingled with her own memories of childhood and Mother, and a cautionary voice in her head warned against the place. She would be too vulnerable there. Suddenly, Vime remembered that Tei had once offered to take her to a place where wild raspberries were always in season. That was the time she had first set eyes on the spirit.

Tei was trying to trap me to that place. Could she have hidden Khrielie there? Vime wondered, her heart racing.

'Hevüsa, do you know a place where wild raspberries are always in season?'

'Hmph . . . no', Hevüsa mumbled, looking away and quite disinterested suddenly. He appeared ready to leave now that he had learnt that Vime was here on her own mission. Vime had heard about the temperamental and unpredictable nature of thekhumiavis. She couldn't afford to lose him. Thinking quickly, Vime blurted a chant which an old grandmother had taught her; one used in times of danger and to appease spirits.

'Hevüsa, Tei Apfu Kijü Apfü; Sky Father Earth Mother. Do you remember? Please help me', Vime pleaded, inwardly hoping that she had not spoken out of context. It was the only thing she could think off.

Hevüsa's grin was wry but he did not look displeased, 'No, Vime. I do not know any such place with ripened raspberries; the raspberries here will never. But the old caretaker of the in-between realms between the human and spirit worlds will know. He has been appointed to look after these places by the old spirits.'

'Where can I find him?' Vime asked, thrilled to finally be getting some concrete answers.

'You will find him by the foot of the bridge over the sorrowing waters. Go to the peripheries of this realm and then jump into the abyss. It will take you to him.'

'Jump? But . . . I went there earlier and felt solid ground. And I couldn't breathe.'

Hevüsa began to speak but was momentarily distracted by a subtle vibration in the air.

'Something is coming', he breathed out, 'You must leave now!' Within seconds, his voice became so thin and reedy that Vime could scarcely hear him. He suddenly looked extremely frail and Vime was amazed that she could see right through him. He's fading right before my very eyes, she realized with horror. Feeling like her fretful heart might just leap out from within the confines of her chest any moment, Vime ran towards the edge of the realm followed by the wispy remains of Hevüsa's memory.

'I wish I could come with you too', whispered Hevüsa when they reached the bordering darkness.

'Come!', Vime urged, thinking how good it would be to have some company while meeting the caretaker of the realms, even if he was a tekhumiavi.

'I can't. I'm a part of this place. This is my wife's memory you are in. Go now Vime, before it's too late. Close your eyes and think of an old man upon a bridge before you jump. That might help', Hevüsa threw a quavering wispy wink as he uttered the words.

Vime wondered how she was going to be able to think of a man and place she had never seen but she nodded obediently.

Turning to him one last time, Vime said hurriedly, 'Thank you, Hevüsa. If ever I return to the living, do you want me to carry a message to your wife?'

Although the outlines of his sheer frame were already dissipating into smoke and wafting up the air, Hevüsa's eyes suddenly grew brilliantly alive, glinting tiger yellow as he answered, 'Tell my wife to let me go, let me rest now. Here, just see that she gets this and she will understand!' Hevusa took off a small cross-body bag on his person and deftly slung the strap diagonally over Vime's shoulders.

Vime turned to the void of darkness and closed her eyes. The last thing she saw before closing her eyes were a pair of tawny amber eyes, slit black irises pulsating, softly glowing against the mist and shadow.

TWENTY-ONE

Vime took a deep breath and with a self-conscious little jump, plunged into the abyss. She half expected to fall on solid ground but her body never made contact. Instead, Vime found herself free falling into an endless vacuum of space as her limbs wildly flailed everywhere, feeling pulled from all directions. Feeling enormously dizzy but trying not to panic, Vime shut her eyes tight and tried to conjure mental images of an old man sitting by the edge of a bridge; the old man in her mind had a kindly face, not unlike her own grandfather.

Suddenly, there was a shift in the centre and Vime felt gravity pull her horizontally. Feeling disjointed, she opened her eyes and it was as if the universe had shifted. Vime found herself floating over endless cascading hills and meadows with the sun, a crescent moon, Saturn and bright stars underneath the waters. A serene peaceful stillness pervaded; time seemed to have stopped in this place and the slow captivating sight made Vime forget all her fears. She felt the sharp stabbings of regret as she involuntarily passed the sublime realm of watery skies and rolling valleys. Very soon, there was nothing, only darkened fog and a different quality of silence—deafening.

Mercifully, however, the silence was abruptly broken by the faint laughter of children and a collective chorus of murmuring adults. The laughter faded as the darkness eased and Vime could see another distant sight below. There were soldiers, young and old, waving flags of stars and rainbows. They were singing a song and although the words were muffled, their song filled Vime with bittersweet sadness—a sadness so profound, like she had just discovered the irrevocable loss of something precious but she knew not what. Vime noted that it was the same flag that she had seen in the place she last saw Mother. She craned her neck below, trying to get a closer look but her body shifted and very quickly, she was no longer unhurriedly floating horizontal but plummeting downwards, crashing past ethereal fields and homes, shadows, strange-looking creatures and faceless people, young and old. It dawned on Vime that she was falling past the many memory realms. Remembering Hevüsa's advice, Vime instinctively folded her arms protectively over her head, closed her eyes again and tried hard to concentrate on the mysterious old caretaker she should have been thinking about this entire time, until she felt her hands gently splash into the soft coolness of water.

Scrambling up her feet, Vime opened her eyes to an endless expanse of shimmering waters underneath a glittering starlit sky. It was difficult to gauge whether the water reflected the skies or the other way round. This must be the sorrowing waters, Vime thought wonderingly. Beyond the shallow waters, she could see white shores with bare trees, the colour of bone. The air in this place was nippy and Vime quickly untied the jacket around her waist and put it on, Hevüsa's bag dangling against her side. Sure enough, just as Hevüsa had described, she could see the distinct curve of a wooden bridge at a distance. At the far end of the bridge stood a gigantic hunched figure and this figure was leaning heavily against a soaring crooked staff which was even taller than its owner, almost like an entire wiry tree had been uprooted. Vime gulped nervously, wondering whether the caretaker belonged to a race of giants. This was an important detail Hevüsa neglected to mention, she thought indignantly.

The bridge was unusual in that instead of land, it began and ended over the shallow waters. Streams of sparkling water lapped and rippled around Vime's feet as she made her way towards the caretaker who appeared oblivious to her presence. His head hung down and he wore a stone-grey robe-like cloak with a hood thrown over, covering him from head to toe. To Vime's astonishment and immense relief, the caretaker who had appeared gigantic from a distance, became increasingly human-sized as she drew closer. When she reached him, he was still a towering figure but by normal human standards.

Vime nervously cleared her throat and spoke, 'Hello, Mr Caretaker Sir. My name is Vime'. Vime's mother had taught her to address all elderly people as 'Apfutsa Grandfather' or 'Atsa Grandmother', out of respect, but she just could not imagine addressing the old caretaker as such. It just seemed incomprehensible.

When the figure did not respond or look up, Vime tried again.

'Hello. Please Mr Caretaker, could you tell me where I can find Khrielie? She's my father's wife', she explained timidly, awkwardly explaining Khrielie's relation to herself.

Vime was shaken when the caretaker finally deigned to look up with a wheeze of laboured breath. She had never seen anyone so old and decrepit-looking. The face that peered at her was gaunt and bloodless pale, liberally lined with stringy wrinkles and spotted with age. His leathery skin appeared tightly stretched over his skull, all the way down an exposed shrivelled neck. It was like staring into a piece of deadened wood with beady black emotionless eyes. Vime almost bolted in fright but she took a deep breath and tried to remain calm. The caretaker's bones creaked as he bent to get a closer look at her.

'You have no business here, human', the caretaker rasped, exhaling puffs of cold vapour as he spoke. Vime thought he looked quite frostbitten.

'No, I don't. But here I am and you are the only one who can direct me to Khrielie', Vime tried to be brave but her voice trembled as she uttered the words.

'I am the caretaker of the in-between and that is all that concerns me', saying this, the caretaker resumed his earlier stance, straightening his posture and hung down his head again.

'Well then, Mr Caretaker, could you please at least direct me to the realm where wild raspberries are always in season?' Vime asked, undeterred. But the old man gave no further response.

Refusing to give up and not knowing what else to do, Vime sat herself down on the bridge beside the caretaker. She looked inside the bag Hevüsa had given her. She did not know what she expected but nevertheless, she was still disappointed to find the bag empty except for an old matchbox with only two matchsticks remaining. However, Vime decided to take hope in the bag. Hevüsa must have given this to me because he believes that I can make it back home, she comforted herself.

Vime did not want to risk annoying the caretaker so she patiently waited for some time before attempting to catch his attention again. But no matter how much she pleaded, cajoled and bargained, the old man remained quite immovable, refusing to acknowledge her presence with neither words nor gesture. If he had not spoken earlier, Vime would have imagined that she was invisible to him. He appeared to not see nor hear her.

'Alright, if you won't help me, I have no choice but to go towards the shores to search for Khrielie myself', Vime finally declared. She may as well have been talking to a block of ice. The only indication that the caretaker had not frozen on the spot was the steady visible puffs of vapour which emitted underneath the hood. Feeling quite chilled herself, Vime suddenly found herself feeling sorry for the old man. Having spent much time with her grandparents, she knew how the elderly were more susceptible to the cold. She imagined how much more comfortable he'd feel if he had a fire to warm his bones. And so, Vime decided to build the caretaker a fire before leaving.

Glad to have a concrete plan for a change, Vime eagerly ran towards the trees on the shores. She was gratified to find plenty of dried twigs and dead leaves fallen on the forest floor. They were all pristine white too, effortlessly blending into the white sand. Vime took off her jacket and bundled inside, as many twigs as she could manage and made her way towards the bridge once more. If the caretaker noticed Vime's earnest activities beside him, he gave no indication of it. Soon, with the providential aid of Hevüsa's matchsticks, Vime was able to kindle a cosy little bonfire on the bridge, just beside the caretaker but carefully positioned away from the cool waters.

'Well, its freezing so I figure this should keep you warm for some time at least. I'll be off then. I'll be in the woods if you change your mind about helping me', Vime said hopefully. With no encouraging sign from the caretaker, she expelled a sad little sigh and began on her way.

As she approached the grove of skeletal trees, she felt a gust of wind and movement behind her. Turning round, Vime was dumfounded at the extraordinary scene unfolding before her. The caretaker was hobbling away towards the opposite direction. As he did so, the lake moved along with him, literally gliding away from the ground. The caretaker's cloak was like an extensive train which floated over and covered the entire reaches of the lake like an all-encompassing fabric. It was only then that Vime realized that the sorrowing waters was none but the old caretaker himself.

Not wanting to lose sight of the caretaker, Vime ran after him as fast as her feet would carry her. When she reached the slow-shifting shoreline, she was dismayed that the depth of the waters was no longer shallow. Her feet sank deeper with every step she took. Vime did not know how to swim but she was nevertheless determined to get to the caretaker. I just need to get to the bridge and I'll be alright, Vime thought frantically. As she doggedly made her way towards the bridge, she found the water quickly rising from her chest towards her chin. She slipped then and went under.

As Vime desperately floundered and flailed underwater, she realized how badly she wanted to live.

TWENTY-TWO

But Vime found that she could not, would not drown. When she finally stopped struggling, she realized that she was breathing underwater, inhaling and exhaling, rhythmically, effortlessly, in and out, streams of tiny bubbles easefully blowing out through her nostrils. A gradual heavy darkness was setting in, and time appeared to slow down as the weight of water pressed heavy against her entire being. Ennui seeped inside Vime's spirit as she felt her fatigued body grow limp while suspended within the heart of the lake. She could hear muted echoes reverberating within the depths of the waters. Drained and depleted of all energy, Vime helplessly closed her eyes and surrendered to the devouring darkness.

It felt that an eternity might have passed before the darkness was broken by blinding white light. It made Vime squint and her hands reflexively covered her eyes against the sudden dazzling radiance.

When her eyes adjusted to the light, she felt her feet grounded and found that she was no longer underneath the water but standing in the middle of a lonely bridge over what now appeared to be a much smaller lake. Vime knew it was the same bridge because the little fire she brought to life by the edge of the bridge was still burning bright. After everything I've witnessed, nothing can surprise me now, thought Vime to herself. The caretaker could no longer be seen in his human form but just as Vime knew it was the same bridge, she also instinctively knew that the lake too was the caretaker, perhaps in his true form. She felt a little silly for having imagined that the old caretaker had felt cold like any ordinary frail human. But she was convinced that she stood here now because of her gesture of kindness, however small it may have been.

Gratified with the knowledge that she had done the right thing, Vime walked to the edge of the bridge, leaned over the wooden rails, stared down deep into the lake and whispered, 'Thank you for not letting me drown.'

After professing gratitude, Vime swore that her reflection over the lake's crystal-clear surface was looking back at her. Her reflection gave a little nod of acknowledgement. Surely a trick of the light or perhaps due to the constant overlapping, coalescing ripples, thought Vime. The idea that her reflection might be communicating with her was incredibly unnerving. Still, Vime could not tear her eyes away from the mesmerizing waters. She rubbed her eyes and looked down again. A gentle breeze briefly disturbed her watery image. When her reflection re-formed, she looked somewhat different. Younger.

As Vime continued to gaze at her watery image, utterly spellbound, she saw herself grow younger and smaller, her life playing backwards in front of her eyes, seemingly contained within the softly undulated waters, morphing from childhood to infancy until the lake finally grew pitch black. The show was over. Still, Vime looked on, feeling completely hypnotized. After what felt like ages, a little watery gyre formed itself in the middle of the lake right under Vime's gaze, rapidly churning, widening and spiralling away from the centre until it spilled over the entire expanse of the lake. Vime thought that the very lake had been overturned. The water was now tranquil; a clear cerulean like the serene blue sky above, leisurely forming watery images once again. This time, however, Vime did not see herself.

It was like the years had fallen away and she was looking into a dream. She saw a modest little house, painted white and bordered with black wooden beams; typically old-fashioned government-allotted housing which her parents referred to as quarters. Although somewhat dilapidated, the little house looked charming with light-pink briar roses growing outside its entrance; petals, thorns and green clinging against the rusty little iron gate. It did not take long for Vime to recognize the old house her family had resided in during the early years, before her father got transferred. Although Vime was a toddler then, too young to remember, some would say, Vime did remember and she knew this was the very same house. Her mother appeared then, looking exceedingly slender and youthful beside her father, who looked boyish and handsome. Vime sensed a third life slowly stirring within mother's bosom and she instinctively knew it had to be Neime. Sure enough, the silhouette of little Neime as a toddler with her trademark mop of curls playfully rippled across the waters. Idyllic images of the young family of three flickered with every watery movement. These were glimpses of her family's life before she was born, and Vime knew that she was peeking into someone else's intimate memories. The waters shivered and trembled suddenly and Vime saw Mother's face—this time older, the way she was when she got sick—grimace in agony while Father held her hands, his eyes reflecting love and pain. After that, Vime could only see her father's face reflected upon the waters; completely alone within a vortex of darkness.

Vime felt her bosom heave and ache with bittersweet sadness and regret for all that had been and was now lost. This time, however, it was for someone else, for everyone rather—Father, Neime, Mother too. For the first time, Vime forgot her own brokenness and felt the suffering of another in a truly visceral way. It made her feel less alone somehow. A profound sense of pathos emanated from the water, so tangible that driven by instinct and forgetting where she was, Vime reached down to touch the desolate faces on the lake. But she couldn't reach down low enough to touch the waters. By now, Vime was leaning precariously over the bridge, standing on the tips of her toes. She grunted and gasped as she attempted to lean down as low as possible without toppling over. As she peered closer into the surface of the lake, she could see beneath the translucent watery reflections. Not too long ago, Vime had believed that she had ceased to be amazed by anything. But once more, she found herself astounded by what she saw.

Vime could actually see the bottom of the lake and it was like nothing she had imagined. Underneath were groves of trees and scattered brambly bushes bearing profusions of bright orange orbs which glowed like lowlights. Fissions of shock went through Vime as she suddenly spotted a familiar-looking figure huddled against a tree. Vime jerked in excitement and the next thing she knew, she was splashing deep into the lake.

She fell into a sun-soaked forest with birds chirping and dark bushes lit with bright tangerine-tinted raspberries. Unable to restrain herself any longer, Vime burst out:

'Khrielie, Khrielie! Where are you? Can you hear me?'

To her pleasant and astonished surprise, an equally baffled Khrielie stepped out from behind a tree, so naturally, as if she had been waiting all along. Finding Khrielie so unexpectedly, Vime felt a tad wary. But the look of cautious joy mingled with wary suspicion on the other girl's face mirrored her own.

Khrielie was almost in tears as she embraced Vime. 'Vime, is it really you? Oh, you clever clever girl. But oh no, we're both trapped here now', Khrielie was trembling, laughing and sobbing all at once.

After reassuring each other that it really was the other person in the flesh, Vime recounted her strange journey to Khrielie. She felt a surge of relief when Khrielie assured her that she had the good sense not to eat raspberries or anything edible-looking in this unnatural place. Khrielie's face became anxious as she emphasized once again how it was only a matter of time before Tei returned. Vime was dismayed when Khrielie informed her that there appeared to be no end to this vast expanse of eternal sunshine and endless raspberry fields.

'But are you sure? Oh, Khrielie, but we have to try to find it. Surely this place must lead somewhere at the very least, even if it is nothingness?'

'Vime, this place is just like Tei. Charming to look at but rotten to the core underneath. I've walked miles only to return to the same spot I started from.'

Nevertheless, refusing to give up and finding renewed strength in each other's presence, Vime and Khrielie searched for the ends of the place but it was futile, like walking an endless path which had neither a beginning nor an end. At least they were able to fill in each other on the way. Vime learned that when she failed to return home in time, Khrielie, feeling both worried and responsible for having convinced Father to allow her to go to school, had gone out to search for her. When she reached the intersection, she had heard Vime call out to her from the woodland.

'I could have sworn it was you. The voice sounded uncannily like you. And you had told me about your frequent sojourns in the forest so I followed the voice until it was too late. Tei had already found me.'

'Khrielie, I'm so sorry for everything. I never wanted to involve you but I missed Apfo desperately and Tei . . . ', Vime felt wretched with guilt and remorse. But Khrielie stopped her as she struggled to explain her actions in the recent past which had led to this moment.

'Assh! No, don't apologize, you don't need to explain even. I can somehow imagine just how charmingly manipulative Tei can be. All that matters is that you came searching for me. That's all that matters. I know you miss your mother', Khrielie briefly hesitated before continuing, 'Vime, I know I can never replace your mother and I would never try. But I would really like to be friends with you and Neime. Would you consider that?'

Despite the turmoil still churning within, Vime felt a heavy burden lifted as relief washed over her. She and Khrielie understood each other.

TWENTY-THREE

Vime felt dizzy with hunger and exhaustion as she sat on the grass next to an equally weary Khrielie. They had been exploring, searching a way out for what felt like hours but nothing of the landscape changed regardless of the miles they covered. It was maddeningly eerie. The trail they walked with its pattern of trees, foliage, raspberry bushes, the blinding sunny-yellow sky—everything appeared the same everywhere they went. They didn't know whether the landscape lazily replicated itself everywhere or if they kept returning to the beginning. Finally, the two girls sat slumped against a tree, their optimistic zeal now replaced with frustrated misery. Vime impatiently wiped the beads of perspiration trickling down her forehead with her sleeve. What she'd give for a bath!

'Get a little sleep, Vime. I'll keep watch. Let's get some rest and then maybe find a better place to hide before Tei returns', Khrielie said, nervously looking over her shoulders while patting her lap, inviting Vime to cushion her head and lie down.

The thought of Tei made the hairs on Vime's arms and neck tingle and stand on end. She couldn't believe there was a time when she had voluntarily sought Tei out. 'Khrielie, Hevüsa had mentioned that the old gods are watching. Perhaps if we search for them instead of a place.. .?' Vime began desperately

'No, Vime, no more bargaining with spirits', Khrielie said firmly and Vime grudgingly accepted the sense in it.

'Khrielie, I'm so hungry', Vime complained, allowing herself to feel like a helpless child as Khrielie placed a reassuring arm over her, stroking her hair. In the midst of her misery, having an adult around felt truly comforting.

'When we get home, I'll prepare the best meal you've ever had', Khrielie promised 'What would you like to eat?'

Vime sat up beside Khrielie and repositioned her head on the crook of the older girl's shoulder. Her stomach rumbled as visions of her favourite food tantalizingly floated before her eyes. Vime spoke with her eyes closed, 'I love crispy fried potato wedges. But right now, I'd like to have piping hot fluffy white rice drenched in chicken broth flavoured with garlic, ginger, nietso and dried red chilies!' Famished, she found herself salivating at the thought of a hot chicken meal. 'Apfo used to make the best chicken. Neime's is almost as good as Apfo's', Vime ruefully reflected over her sister's efforts to reproduce their mother's specialties. She had never truly appreciated Neime's efforts until now. Vime suddenly remembered how Mother had once chided them for not getting along, confessing that her lifelong lament had always been that she did not have a sister herself.

Khrielie's voice was quiet as she spoke, 'Mother learnt how to bake when she was a young girl. She rarely bakes as it reminds her of happier times gone by. But when she does, the fragrance of freshly baked cake permeates the entire house, filling it with sunshine and sweetness. She was planning to bring us one of her special cakes.'

'I have a best friend. Khriebu, that's her name. I had planned to invite her home for tea and introduce her to you. A home-baked cake would have been ideal', Vime wistfully mused.

'Apfo Neilaü's daughter?'

Vime nodded.

'She seems nice. What do you and Khriebu like to do together?'

'Oh, everything. We laugh over the silliest things when we're together. She's incredible funny'.

'Hmmm.'

Both girls grew quiet then, each lost in their own thoughts. Vime was the first to break the silence,

'It's funny, isn't it?

'What is?'

'That it's the little things, the mundane boring everyday stuff that binds you to home.'

'You're right', Khrielie agreed, her voice soft and pensive.

What's your favourite thing to do?' Vime asked, sitting up straight and turning to look into Khrielie's open face. Oddly enough, she was enjoying their banter, despite their hopeless situation. It was remarkably easy to talk to Khrielie.

With a dreamy smile, Khrielie folded her knees against her chest and rested her head as she spoke, 'Hmm . . . My favourite thing. I like sleeping.' She sounded so very sincere and serious that Vime responded with a most unladylike snort of laughter.

'Sleeping?! Is that truly your favourite thing to do!' Vime exclaimed incredulously, her voice dripping with disdain. Khrielie guffawed over Vime's obvious scorn and soon, the two girls were sharing fits of laughter, weary misery further compounding their mirth.

Suddenly, angry thunder rumbled and the drearily bright ceiling passing for sunlit skies filled with what sounded like a distant cacophony of dissent. Vime and Khrielie swiftly got up their feet and looked up. Although they could see nothing other than sky, the gathering mayhem above effectively sobered them, wiping all trace of merriment.

'Shuush Vime, I don't think the old spirits appreciate the sound of our laughter', Khrielie whispered as the skies continued to swell with sounds of disgruntlement. Vime nodded. That made sense, she thought, as the old spirits seemed to take their places of memoriam very seriously.

Ceaseless thunder and lightning contrasted against the serene backdrop of sunny skies was unreal. The two girls stood with their backs protectively against each other, spines stiff with tension and looking around them uncertainly.

'Do you think this fracas might alert Tei?' Vime shouted anxiously as the rumbling dissent reached a deafening crescendo and with it, a gathering of dark clouds overhead.

Khrielie did not answer. Instead, she wordlessly reached out and gripped Vime's hand, tense and alert, as the air became charged with electricity. Khrielie only needed to look at Vime.

'Tei?' Vime mouthed fearfully, already knowing the answer. She had hoped that they would be able to find a way out before Tei returned but it was too late now.

'Hold me tight! Whatever happens, we will not allow Tei to separate us!' Khrielie exclaimed.

Vime and Khrielie hugged each other tightly as they spotted a suspicious speck in the sky which became dreadfully and increasingly familiar as it drew closer. Vime could feel Khrielie's heart beat frantically against her chest, or perhaps it was her own, she couldn't be sure.

'One for two, two for one, trapped eternally in the in-between', the wind whistled; sweet, melodic and unmistakably Tei.

A figure, slight but conspicuous, suspended itself over them. It was Tei. The darkened skies had obstructed her from view until now. Tei landed gracefully, the tip of her toes lightly grazing the ground. But there was nothing graceful about her expression. A diabolic smirk played on Tei's face and nothing could disguise the restrained malevolence on her face. It was horrifying, how her expression contained both malicious glee and fury together.

Vime and Khrielie felt the unnatural wind against their backs, nudging them towards Tei. Driven by gut instinct, they turned to run, hand in hand, sweaty palms and racing hearts, towards the opposite direction of the wind which now blew harshly against them, pelting their faces with bits of earth and gravel. The skies became darker and it was getting hard to see where they were going; moreover, everywhere sinisterly appeared the same. Vime briefly paused to take in their surroundings and was rewarded with an unfamiliar sight which made her heart leap in elation.

'Khrielie, look there, see those houses? Let's go there!' Vime exclaimed excitedly. Beyond, a short distance away, stood a valley with a cluster of houses nestled within. Most

of the houses were hidden by sloping hills running through
and around, but their roof tops could be seen. Bizarrely,
neither Khrielie nor Vime had seen this place until now.
There was no time to waste, none for further discussion; any
place away from Tei was a better idea so the girls frantically
ran towards the mysterious valley which appeared to have
sprung out of nowhere.

Tei was gaining in, her song clearer and sweeter than
ever and all the more sinister because of it. Against her
will, Vime felt a thrill in her heart and she found herself
involuntarily singing along; she just knew every note, each
key. Vime realized later that she must have stood transfixed
because she remembered Khrielie looking at her in horror
and roughly tugging at her arm, urging her to keep moving.
Vime heard Tei's song chase after them until it abruptly
ended with an outraged snarl and the sound of the gnashing
of teeth. She had to cover her ears to still the painfully jarring
noise. Only after the song had ceased, did Vime realize that
the gnashing of teeth was her own.

As they drew closer to the valley, the skies calmed and
they could no longer hear any lingering trace of Tei's song
in the air; in fact, it was like the valley was created under a
different sky. Nevertheless, the sky still grew dim, and mist
and shadow steadily took over until they could no longer
see anything in their path.

TWENTY-FOUR

The temperature dropped and the air felt cooler here, wherever they had come. It was still pitch-dark but they were relieved that they could no longer sense Tei's presence. Engulfed in gloomy stillness, Vime imagined this was what midnight would be like without the moon and stars to give light and comfort. It was a lonely thought. Arms tensely locked, the two girls stumbled onwards awkwardly until they felt their feet move upwards and they knew that they must be walking up a slope. Finally, overcome by fatigue, they stopped to rest. Still holding on to each other's arms, Vime and Khrielie soon fell into exhausted sleep.

Vime was woken by the distant but distinct sound of war-cries. It sounded like armies of warrior tribes getting ready to engage in battle. However, she couldn't make out the direction where the pandemonium originated. It seemed to come from everywhere like restless wandering echoes.

'Vime, do you hear that?' Khrielie whispered fearfully.

Vime nodded, wide awake, forgetting that Khrielie could not see her. Thankfully, dawn was breaking, abnormally swift, just like nightfall had set in, not too long ago. Vime wasn't sure if she could tell day or night apart in this extraordinary place, if there were days or nights at all; just someone switching on and off paranormal lights. But it soon became bright enough to see that they were on the crest of a low hill.

'Look, down there! The houses we saw last night. Let's go there', Khrielie exclaimed breathlessly. Sure enough, a cluster of houses, shacks rather, huddled close by. The little houses circled themselves around the biggest house which appeared to be a Morung, a community dormitory hall, with its typically high-pitched elongated roof. It was like a small community had neatly settled themselves in the heart of a valley of hills.

As they made their way down, Vime first noticed Khrielie's and then her own bare skin. The skies were muted kaleidoscope hues and it painted everything it touched. Their clothes and skin appeared a forlorn blue-green and as enigmatic as the skies above.

'Hello, vorzie ho', Khrielie called out uncertainly as they approached the open door of the first house they met. A hen and few chickens clucked nearby, and on the ground was unhusked rice spread on a mat to be dried by a non-existent sun. There was not a soul to be seen, however.

This place seemed deserted except that all the houses appeared well-maintained and showed signs of being presently occupied. Well-fed chickens contentedly clucked about, the odd cow and pigs wandered and fireplaces were lit. There were looms outside a few patios with the loose yarn half woven, all of which Khrielie, a skilled weaver herself, inspected. Vime did not know anything about weaving but Khrielie remarked that it was intriguing how identical shawls were in the process of being woven on all the looms.

Khrielie exclaimed admiringly, 'Vime, I have never in my life seen such fine work. Come closer and look at this!' Khrielie urged, excitement making her bold.

As Vime cautiously leaned in, Khrielie pointed to the intricate motifs on a half-woven shawl and explained, 'You know, in the old days, people were very careful about their clothing because the fabric tells something about the wearer and is a form of identity expression. Stories were told through weaves and motifs. Shawls like these could denote the social status—wealth, rank, prowess or bravery of its wearer, even the environment that surrounds the wearer, you know? The relationship with the environment and with each other', Khrielie finished triumphantly.

'So, what kind of shawl is this?' Vime asked, idly curious, still apprehensively looking over her shoulders now and then.

'I'm not quite sure as it's still not completed . . . ', as Khrielie gingerly lifted the fabric for a closer inspection, a lone innocuous white little cowrie shell loosened and fell into a wooden bowl filled to the brim with cowries.

'Goodness Vime! This must be for a warrior!' Seeing Vime's blank perplexed stare, Khrielie explained hurriedly, 'Only warriors can have cowries decorated on their shawls. All the shawls here must be intended for warriors or important men at least.'

Vime suddenly remembered the war cries they had heard, 'Khrielie, don't you think we should leave now?'

'We're here, Vime, let's just have a quick look inside the Morung. Maybe we can find someone or something there', Khrielie insisted, walking ahead while Vime followed, a little reluctantly.

As the two girls approached the bared entrance of the huge dormitory hall, they nervously paused before entering. An immense wooden mural hung down the middle of the doorway and the wood was adorned with astral figures, perplexing reptilic animals, mithuns and hornbill feathers, fierce warriors holding human heads on one hand and wielding spears on the other. Vime wordlessly glanced at Khrielie and saw her own nervousness reflected back. They could hear what sounded like an old woman's voice, humming a thepfhe, the kind of songs that young peli groups sang while working the fields. However, this melody was unique in that the singer ended the repetitive tune by ululating the customary wei, the distinctive war cry made by warriors after slaying a victim. The voice sounded like it belonged to one who might have once had a beautiful voice but had now been coarsened with age.

'Grandmother, Atsa, vorzie ho', Khrielie called out, her throat dry and her voice sounding uncharacteristically but understandably timid.

The song paused.

'Lerlie', returned a rasping voice, inviting them to enter quite calmly, unsurprisingly, as if they were expected all along.

The inside of the dormitory was bigger than they had imagined and the roof was so high up that their eyes couldn't meet the ceiling. Indeed, but for the roof they had seen outside, it would seem that there was no ceiling at all, only infinite space above.

The massive hall was empty except for a lone weaver on her loom on the far end. She had her back towards them and was singing as she wove. The weaver sang in the same grating voice they heard outside and her song fell into a lingering imperceptible hum as they drew closer. They couldn't see her face but her scrawny bare shoulders and arms appeared leathery and mottled, and her hunched posture betrayed old age. Unmindful of their presence, the old weaver effortlessly continued drawing in, out, up, down, employing her weaving tools jükrie, jülei, khuthu sei, jüpou, all at once, like an elaborate orchestra, almost as if she had an extra pair of invisible hands to work with. There were all varieties of tree barks, cotton and nettles methodically piled into little mountains on the floor, all evidences indicating that the woman was making her own yarn and threads from scratch. Vime glanced sideways at Khrielie, imagining how impressed the older girl must be. Sure enough, Khrielie's jaw hung down, looking utterly spellbound.

Since their presence appeared to be known, they obsequiously waited, hesitant, not interrupting, until the old weaver calmly ceased her weaving. She continued humming as she detached herself from the loom, her gait unsteady as she reached for a walking stick and finally turned around to face them. To their astonishment, the weaver had the face of a young woman, certainly no older than Khrielie herself. She had a tattoo, the black markings precise and beautifully etched on her smooth youthful chin, indicating that she had participated in victory rituals after a battle.

Khrielie was about to speak, ready to address the woman as Atsa, Grandmother, again, but the weaver's unexpected

youthful visage rendered her speechless. The woman
appeared all-knowing and chortled, making herself cough
and wheeze in the process.

Vime recovered faster. By now, she understood how
deceptive appearances could be. She had a feeling that the
youthful face was a façade and spoke thus: 'Atsa, can you
please tell us where we are?'

The old woman shrewdly appraised Vime with
narrowed eyes and confirmed what they had suspected, and
feared all along, 'This is the warrior's village.'

They both wondered where all the warriors were but
felt it better not to know.

'Atsa, can you please help us return to our human
world?' Khrielie asked.

'Why did you come here then? I did not invite you.'

'We had no choice. It was either here or Tei, and
we chose this place as we needed to escape Tei who
had tricked us into the in-between', Khrielie rambled
desperately. At Khrielie's words, the woman threw Vime a
quick side glance, an amused glint in her alert all-knowing
eyes. Vime blushed and felt she might not like this old
woman too much.

'Know that this place cannot be chosen like any ordinary
destination. No human nor spirit can enter my village
without my knowledge or consent. This place exists as and
when I will it', the weaver haughtily stated. Vime found it a
curious task to reconcile the woman's youthful face and aged
voice. The woman's countenance appeared conceited as she
spoke but her gravelly and raucous voice simply sounded
calm and quite matter-of-fact. She wondered which one
the weaver really was.

'Atsa, as you said, no one can come here without your consent. Is that really so different from inviting us? We wouldn't be here unless you wanted us to be.' The old woman threw a sharp look as Vime sulkily mumbled the last words. Khrielie hastily took over.

'Please Atsa, we appreciate your kindness in letting us in, else we would be in Tei's clutches by now. But we can't stay, we need to get home. Our family will be worried sick about us.'

Without bothering to reply, the weaver leisurely walked around them, picked up some loose yarn and elegantly wound it around her long-tapered fingers into a ball. She appeared to enjoy making them wait for a response. Finally, still looking quite unbothered and rather bored, the weaver stooped to pick a rather splendid looking tree-bark, solid and crusty, kept apart from the rest. She held it against her chest as though it were something precious. The youthful face of the old weaver radiated pleasure as she addressed Vime and for the first time, both her physiognomy and voice synched. Vime could finally believe that both belonged to the same owner.

'Tell Kijübode that I have done as he asked. I have protected you from Tei. No human has ever set foot here before you and none ever will again. You may leave now. But this is the warrior's village and you will have to go through Chüsenu.'

Saying this, the old weaver sat back down and resumed her weaving. She closed her eyes as she wove and began to croon a haunting tune which sounded ancient and terrible, sending icy shivers down Vime and Khrielie's spines. The old weaver now seemed wrapped in a world of her own, unapproachable and oblivious to their presence, almost as if the heart-rending song had engulfed her. Not knowing what else to do, Vime and Khrielie backed away uncertainly and made their way towards the exit.

TWENTY-FIVE

Although there was no wind, the door of the Morung slammed shut by itself as they approached the exit.

'Push harder', groaned Khrielie until she finally managed to push her deft work-hardened fingers inside the gap and prised open the heavy wooden door. The door promptly shut behind them with a dull thud the moment they stepped outside, making them jump.

Eerie silence cloaked the entire village like a thick heavy blanket. The time, the place appeared truly deserted; not a creature was to be seen. The darkened skies, now devoid of colour, looked ready to burst open. A low storm was brewing. Just then, a blood-curdling ululation rang out, followed by a blinding flash of razor-sharp lightning. In that brief moment of white-hot illumination, they saw, from a distance, the approaching silhouettes and shadows of fierce warriors with towering spears that touched the heavens.

'We have to get out of here before the warriors return', Vime and Khrielie both exclaimed in unison, hearts racing, as they ran towards the opposite direction, as fast as their feet could carry them. Khrielie slipped and tumbled once and Vime had to run back for her even as the older girl shouted that she was alright and for Vime to keep moving. The girls ran until they were quite out of breath and were compelled to slow down. Bent over, with a hand pressed to her stomach, Khrielie panted and wheezed in pain as she rested her other hand against the trunk of a tree for support. Vime too helplessly rested her weight against a tree, feeling stomach cramps building.

They looked around. Wherever they were, the black marshy earth in this place was cold and damp, as if it had never known the goodness of sunshine and warmth. No creature, fern or flower, nothing of beauty could be seen except for the twisted gargantuan trees which loomed above them, austere and forbidding; it made them feel vulnerable and insignificant. Even the air in this forest felt dank and musty; they had the ominous sense that they were on unchartered territory.

'Khrielie, what did the old weaver mean when she said we have to pass through Chüsenu?' Vime whispered fearfully.

Khrielie's throat felt dry and her nervous gulp was audible. She looked around, her eyes fearfully wide and alert, not looking at Vime as she spoke:

'My grandfather used to speak of it. It's an ancient prophecy referring to a battlefield in the deepest untouched woods where war will take place, towards the end of days.'

'War between whom?'

'I don't know, Vime. Prophecies always seem vague to me.'

'Are we in Chüsenu?' Vime whispered. Uneasy silence seemed to stretch and reverberate before Khrielie could breathe an answer.

'I think so, Vime.'

'But it's not the end of days yet, is it...Is it?' Vime repeated when Khrielie failed to answer.

'I've told you everything I know, Vime', Khrielie said testily, which was quite unlike her sweet nature.

'Well, I don't think it is. And anyway, the warriors' shawls are still in the process of being woven. I don't think the battle will take place now. The old weaver just said we have to go through Chüsenu, so let's just cross this place then', Vime said, arguing with herself, desperately trying to reassure them both.

'Let's hope you're right', Khrielie sighed wearily.

The deeper they walked into the woods, the lesser they felt—their insides increasingly hollow, as if the forest was devouring their spirit inside out. For some reason, this place evoked bitter thoughts and Vime's mind agitatedly buzzed with unpleasant recollections. She couldn't stop thinking about Father and his inconsiderate tactless ways, how he had turned hers and Neime's life upside down. She first grew furious then felt her heart grow heavy and cold; a slow rising despair was threatening to overwhelm her until she felt almost claustrophobic, like the forest were crushing her.

'Khrielie, I don't feel so good.'

Khrielie listlessly stopped to glance at Vime, her complexion pallid and lips devoid of colour, mirroring Vime's restless lethargy.

'I don't know if this place is better than facing Tei. Why would Kijübode send us here?' Vime petulantly thought aloud, irritated with Kijübode and everything around her.

'What do you expect from a brainless tree?' Khrielie bit out, uncharacteristically short-tempered. Her mouth rounded in surprise the moment the words came out and she looked mortified with her own tetchiness.

'Oh, Vime, I'm so sorry', Khrielie apologized but Vime brushed her apology with a dismissive wave. She was too sick to take offence and moreover, she knew it wasn't Khrielie really. There was just something rotten about this place which infected all that came in contact with it.

Wordless and heartsick, they stopped to rest. Khrielie sat down, resting her back against a violently jagged tree and gestured for Vime to lie down beside her. The swampy earth felt clammy but Vime rested her head upon Khrielie's folded lap and gradually drifted to a deep restless sleep, her breath laboured and unsteady as she slept.

And she dreamt.

Vime dreamt of the night and being back on her beloved cobbled footpath. The world had gone to sleep; all was calm. Guiding and lighting her path were tiny fireflies, fluttering luminous against the canvas of dark night. Dead souls on their way to the afterlife, Vime thought, remembering an old, much-loved song. All fatigue had vanished and Vime felt very much alert. She was awake in a dream.

And Vime knew she really was dreaming when she saw Mother. Mother looked different; ethereal, her body radiating incandescent light from within, not younger like in the in-between, not older either, but like she was finally resting in her true form. But when Mother spoke, her voice sounded exactly like the way Vime remembered—earthy, jovial. I must remember to tell Neime this; that people sound exactly like themselves in the afterlife, thought Vime.

Mother smiled, as if she knew what Vime was thinking. They walked together, side by side. After waking, Vime would not remember all they spoke of. But she would remember telling Mother how beautiful she looked.

'Apfo, so much has happened after you left. Neime is in college now.'

'I know, Vime, I know.'

'Father remarried.'

'Yes, I know', Mother smiled kindly, 'Is she nice?'

'She's very nice', Vime thought she'd feel guilty saying this but she didn't. She knew Mother understood.

'And you? How are you?' Mother asked, her eyes shining bright with boundless limitless love.

'I wasn't okay for a long time. But I'm going to be alright now', Vime felt happy and sad too as she spoke her heart.

'That's my brave clever girl. I'm so proud of you.'

'Oh, Apfo, I miss you, I've missed you so much.'

'I know Vime. And I have, you. But now you know that I'm still with you somehow. Do you remember how I have prayed for you and Neime, and Father? My prayers are alive now, more than ever . . . ', Mother's voice was achingly tender, filled with so much love that Vime felt herself immersed in something indescribably pure, joyous and infinitely powerful.

'My brave Vime, live boldly, embrace the world, drink the sea, take it all in, and be so very happy', Mother whispered with a soft feathery light kiss on the cheek which woke Vime. Her eyes opened to Chüsenu and Khrielie dozing restlessly. Vime wasn't sad that it was a dream. She knew now that dreams were glimpses into the wondrous unknown. All fears evaporated and she felt a lightness of heart she had never experienced in all the entirety of her young life.

TWENTY-SIX

'K hrielie, wake up, wake up, I have an idea', Vime shook the older girl whose eyes were closed. But Khrielie wasn't asleep really.

'What is it?' Khrielie uninterestedly opened her eyes. Vime was struck with Khrielie's appearance but didn't say anything. Her already pale complexion was wan and flaxy, her hair limp and her eyes looked appallingly vacant and empty.

Vime lightly patted Khrielie's cheeks to shake the sluggishness out of her. 'Khrielie, I have an idea. Listen', Vime leaned in to whisper because she did not trust this place. 'Remember when we were laughing in that previous place and we thought that the old spirits did not like our laughter and that we seemed happy? I think there's something there. Hevüsa told me that the old spirits will not intervene unless something threatens the existence of these realms. Don't you see? These physical paeans are sacred memorials to them. Grandfather Kijübode told me that only those who have lost all love for life can stay here.

We have to compel the spirits to banish us from here. We must show them that we don't belong here.'

Vime felt quite out of breath when she finished. She had never spoken so much so fast and she had not been as succinct as she'd like. But it was enough. Khrielie dumbly stared at Vime for a few seconds before comprehension slowly infused colour and light back into her face. Vime thought it was marvellous what even the tiniest grain of hope could do.

'How do we do this?'

The two girls first tried laughing but their forced purposeful laughter felt hollow and they realized they'd need to do better to convince the old spirits. But Vime wasn't perturbed in the least. She knew just what to do.

'Khrielie, forget all else. Close your eyes and think of home and all things good and wonderful', Vime urged.

Vime and Khrielie looked at each other in silent determination, drawing strength from each other. Vime confidently squeezed Khrielie's hand and then closed her eyes first.

Imagine a panoramic view—a forbidden pre-creation forest as old as time, hostile trees rooted upon an earth which knew no laughter or sunshine, only bitter ghostly memories, all waiting to fulfill an ancient prophecy, and somewhere within this bleak emptiness, two young girls lying on their backs, hand in hand, as if on a gay picnic, lips delicately curved upwards, with tremulous tranquil smiles.

Vime imagined being home with Father, Neime and Khrielie, safe under one roof.
The comfort of her clean soft bed and plush pillows

A mug of steaming hot milk with a good storybook
to read
Looking out the window during blustery rainy days
That wonderful feeling after a warming hot bath
The smell of fresh earth after rain
The way grass tickles bare feet
Supper time and all the delicious things to eat
Sharing laughter and secrets with Khriebu
Visiting her grandparents in the village
Fragrant guavas and wildflowers near the fields
The sound of laughter and warmth of sunshine
Lazy Sunday afternoons with nothing to do
Strolling down her very own sunlit cobbled footpath
School and how much she had to catch up on. Vime's
eyelids twitched as she involuntarily murmured
aloud, 'Oh, I must get notes from Khriebu.'

Her dreams of travelling the world came to mind. She had
so much to do with her life still. Hadn't she promised her
mother to be a good girl and obey Father and Neime, too?
Memories of Neime and Father and her doting grandparents
flooded through her mind. How worried they must be right
now. She had to live not only for herself but for those who
loved her.

Vime felt hot tears streaming down her cheeks, lost
within a floodgate of reverie, until she felt Khrielie shake her
back to reality. Khrielie's voice sounded nervously jubilant.

'Vime, Vime, look! I think it's working!'

Vime opened her eyes to discover that the forest
around them was slowly disintegrating into dust and
grey nothingness, dissolving before her very eyes. Grainy

gargantuan figures hovered above while wraithlike spectres flitted back and forth in agitated movements. A cacophony of murmuring dissent reverberated across the width and length of infinite space, becoming increasingly louder until pandemonium broke.

'Who brought them here', a low voice thundered from above.

'They cannot stay and pollute the sacred realms!' another voice boomed.

Smoke and shadows merged to form a gigantic grimacing face which loomed down low, closer and closer until it was right above the two cowering girls. What passed for solid ground gave way just then and the last thing Vime recalled was the shadow's enormous mouth open and swallow them whole.

They were floating, suspended in pitch darkness. Vime felt Khrielie's hand slipping away from hers even as she tried to cling on to the latter's sweaty slippery fingers. But despite her best efforts, Vime felt herself pulled away towards the opposite direction. She opened her mouth to scream but no sound came out. It was so dark and dizzying that after some time, Vime could no longer tell whether her eyes were open or closed. And so, Vime stopped struggling and simply thought of home.

TWENTY-SEVEN

Vime felt herself free falling and woke with a start. The dazzling warmth of daylight flooded her face, making her feel light-headed and giddy. She was lying flat on her back and it took several seconds for the blurry visages hovering above to take focus. Father's expressive dark eyes underneath his deeply furrowed brows looked worried. Another head almost touching Father's was a woman with a white cap perched on top. She also recognized their local pastor standing in between, beaming and looking unusually serene.

'Ah, she's up finally! Vime, how do you feel?' asked the nurse.

'Khrielie's up! She's fine!', Khrielie's mother barged inside the tiny hospital room to discover Vime sitting up, being checked by the nurse.

'Most curious', observed the doctor later as everyone marvelled over how both Vime and Khrielie had regained consciousness on the dot, right to the very second. The doctor checked both patients and declared that aside from some weight loss, they were in the best of health. As for what had happened, he admitted that he was completely flummoxed, declaring that he had never witnessed anything like this in his twenty-five years of experience in the medical profession.

Later, Vime learned that when Khrielie did not return with her, Father had set out to search for both of them. To his horror, he had found Vime unconscious, lying face down beside the cobbled footpath which led to the forest, her school books spilling down the steps. Khrielie was also found in a similar state just a few metres away from Vime. Father had rushed them both to the nearby hospital where they had remained unconscious for five days. Although their vitals appeared normal, when the girls remained insensible even on the fourth day, Father in desperation, had asked the pastor to come and pray for them.

When Vime narrated what had happened to her, Father looked incredulous and also skeptical at the same time.

'That's quite a dream, my girl. You should write about it!' he remarked dryly. But his slackened jaws and grim expression betrayed conflicting emotions; bewildered disbelief mingled with concern. Vime felt exceedingly frustrated over the trace of doubt which tinged Father's words.

'Didn't Khrielie tell you the same thing? How can both of us have the exact same dream?' Vime challenged him.

'It would be arrogance to deny the existence of the supernatural world. But rest assured, God is always there to protect His children', the pastor simply remarked, blessing them before departing.

Listening to Khrielie and Vime recount their shared experience in precise minute detail, Neime and Khrielie's elderly mother's eyes widened in fear and wonderment, while Father appeared quite dumbfounded. When Vime told them about Hevüsa's bag which should have been on her person, Neime promptly got up and within seconds, returned with a little woven bag in her hand. It had been on Vime when father found her unconscious. Neime had taken it off her at the hospital and had kept it safe.

'Yes! This is the bag. I have to give it to his wife. Might anyone know her?' Vime asked.

Khrielie's mother spoke; 'I've heard of the widow Vikho whose late husband was rumored to be a thekhumiavi. She lives with her young son in Pezielietsie area. But based on what I've heard, her husband possessing a tiger spirit is something she has never publicly acknowledged.'

Father suddenly interrupted; 'Wait! Vime, didn't you say that you met Hevüsa towards the later part of your journey?'

'Yes.'

'So how would it be possible that it was already on you when I found you within the early hours of your absence? Mind you, we had begun searching early on since we had already learned that all the schools had been closed. Listen Vime, could it be possible that you had dreamt the entire thing?' Father began, his eyes and tone cautiously hopeful. It would make everything a lot simpler.

Khrielie intervened: 'You are discounting our entire experience based on a technicality. Anyway, I don't believe that time in the paranormal world is linear like we understand it in the physical human world.'

Father finally accepted, reluctantly, that something extraordinary had indeed happened to Vime and Khrielie.

In the days to come, however, Father discouraged them from 'reliving their most disturbing adventure', as he put it, by talking about it more than they ought to.

'What matters is that both of you are home safe. Let's not talk about this anymore, no need to give the unexplained more power than necessary by dwelling on it, and let's never discuss this with other people, alright?' Father insisted firmly, covering all angles, much to Vime's disappointment.

Father had forbidden Vime from seeking out Hevüsa's widow (she will think you are crazy or worse, you might only end up hurting her, Father insisted) or going to the forest, which Vime felt was to be expected. However, he eventually relented upon the latter when Vime would not stop pleading to be allowed to say a proper thank you to Grandfather Kijübode.

Hand in hand, Vime felt Father's grip tighten as they neared the end of the cobbled footpath on a crisp winter morning. She wanted to reassure him, tell him it was alright but she thought that would only make him even more nervous. The forest behaved itself that day, serene even, the calm ever so often broken by a screech and other usual forest sounds. The bamboo trees danced in the wind and Vime's heart gave a little twitch as she remembered Tei. But she just didn't feel susceptible anymore. Too much had happened and she was a different person now.

When they reached, Vime thought Grandfather Kijübode looked as majestic as ever. He did not wear a face that day but that was to be expected. 'It's alright, Father', Vime said, urging Father to let go of her hand. As Father patiently waited, Vime approached the tree. She had rehearsed what to say, but suddenly, words seemed miserably inadequate. Driven by a surge of pure joy, she threw open her arms, as wide as she could manage, and hugged Grandfather Kijübode. Vime closed her eyes in wordless gratitude and imagined Grandfather Kijübode was returning her embrace, calling her Young Vime once more. It truly seemed like it, as despite the chilly weather, the tree felt incredibly warm and comforting.

On their way back home, Vime suddenly stopped to hug Father, burying her face against his chest.

'Now what was that for?' Father asked awkwardly but affectionately stroking her hair, looking surprised but immensely pleased all the same.

'No reason. I'm just happy', Vime replied before taking his hand again.

Father dropped Vime off at Khriebu's house and insisted on picking her up later. He was still fearful of letting Vime off by herself.

'Now I will be back here before dinner time, alright? Wait for me to come and get you. Under no circumstances are you to leave this house by yourself, do you understand? Not even with Khriebu', Father sternly reminded a final time before departing.

When Vime appeared a tad embarrassed over what she perceived as her Father's over-protectiveness, Khriebu quickly came to his defence.

'Can't say I blame him, considering all that's happened. Vime, you should have seen yourself lying unconscious on the hospital bed. It was unreal; you looked appalingly pale and you'd be breathing normally but every now and then, your breath would turn all shallow and you'd shiver and exhale vapour then, although the room was warm enough and you had heaps of blanket over you. Seeing you so helpless and not knowing what was wrong was awful to watch. My mother burst into tears the moment she saw you. Not to cry and make things worse was all anyone could do, really. I felt especially bad for your father the last time Mother and I visited', Khriebu explained, describing how her father had been sleeping upon an uncomfortable wooden bench beside Vime in the hospital room.

'Yes, well, anyway tell me about your uncle. Is he alright?' Vime asked, feeling a little guilty and changing the subject.

'Yes. Tell you a secret. But first . . . ', Khriebu prompted.

'Cross my heart, hope to die', Vime promised solemnly, a hand over her heart.

'Uncle sent word that his battalion is on their way somewhere far away for military training. On foot. They will have already reached the Northern Command at Mon now. He didn't specify where they are going but Mother thinks it will be either China or Pakistan as that's where our soldiers have gone to undergo training previously. Vime, promise that you will remember to pray for the safe return of Uncle and his friends.'

Vime promised, thinking back to the only time she had seen Khriebu's uncle, trying to remember his features and what he looked like, but she couldn't, as his face had been eclipsed by the shadow of his hand.

'I gave Uncle the lucky stone, Vime. I hope that's alright', Khriebu said happily. 'Vime, why is that stone special? Did you find it in the in-between?' Khriebu's guileless eyes widened in hopeful anticipation as she asked her question.

'No Khriebu, it's a stone I found on the intersection, the main road above your house. Or maybe the stone found me. But I just know it's special. You just have to believe it is.'

TWENTY-EIGHT

'Now, you are a hundred and ten percent positive this is her house, right?' Vime asked for the umpteenth time.

'Yes Vime. Now will you please hurry? The woman will appear any moment now', Neime whispered loudly, nervously, feeling extremely conspicuous.

Ever since her return, a persistent guilt which niggled Vime was the fact that Hevüsa's bag was still with her. One day, she confided to Neime who seemed to understand how she felt. Together, the sisters made a secret plan to hang the bag on the little wooden gate outside the widow's house while she was away. Vime carefully adjusted the strap around the gatepost one final time before allowing Neime to drag her away finally.

'Do you think I'll get a chance to meet her one day and tell her about her husband?' Vime asked hopefully

'I know you will. Just not today', Neime promised.

On the way home, the two girls stopped to gather wild orchids for Mother's grave. Armed with a bouquet of blue vandas, it struck Vime that the old dread which used to gnaw at her, deepening the hollow in her heart each time she faced the prospect of returning to a home without Mother had eased. Nowadays, missing Mother had become the dull throb of an old wound. She knew it would never leave. But that was quite alright; it was only love undying.

What had happened sometimes felt like a dream, that too someone else's dream, not her own. Perhaps that's why Vime found herself often wanting to discuss the shared adventure with Khrielie. She didn't want to forget. But as time passed, the need for validation soon waned in light of knowing her truth. Our Vime was growing up.

Who knows what wonders life holds for each of us? And how do we make sense when so many voices clamour to explain life's unexpected turns. One day, after finishing her homework, Vime thoughtfully looked out her room window, journal and a pen in hand. It was turning dusk, a time of day when the light grew softer and the world turned slower in small towns. Outside, she could see weary farmers returning home from the fields, their backs laden with the familiar khorüs, while the little paan and sweet shops strewn along the length of road were, too, beginning to close. As Vime flipped her journal, a gentle gust of wind suddenly blew open the page where the lavender wildflower from the in-between lay tucked. The little flower had now begun to dry and wither like any normal plant. Vime carefully picked it up, twirling the deceptively delicate stem between her thumb and index finger. She recalled her astonishment in the initial days after her return when she first discovered that the flower was still perfectly intact, fresh and lovely, as if it had just awoken. Her first impulse had been to rush down with it, to display it as a token of proof for her skeptics. But just then, something made her hesitate and then change her mind consequently. It didn't matter, Vime had decided as she kept back the flower between the pages. In the years to come, Vime's adventure would not always hold under humankind's amusing propensity to insist on making sense of things that are beyond frail human understanding. And in failing to do so, deny themselves a glimpse into the marvellous unknown. But at that moment, as Vime held the curious little flower in the palm of her hand, she realized two things. One, that unfortunate is the person whose imagination does not take flight when it meets with the unknown. And that as long as she, Vime, believed in her truth, well, that was all there was to it really, she decided.

Vime once asked Neime, 'You never doubted my story even once, did you?'

'No' Neime had replied without hesitation.

'Why?'

Neime thought a while and carefully answered, thinking as she spoke, 'I don't know. At first, I thought who would believe you if not your sister. But then later, it felt like you came back a different person; like someone who's been on a long journey and has finally found a way home.'

Vime put down the flower and closed the journal. As she continued to look out the window, reflecting, ruminating, she heard Father's heavy footsteps towards her bedroom door followed by his signature double knock.

'Come in, it's open', Vime called out and sat on her bed, facing the door.

Father pulled up a chair, seated himself beside her and took out a brown envelope tucked inside his shirt pocket.

Without a word, Father solemnly placed the envelope on the bed. He chuckled appreciatively as Vime threw him a suspicious look as she opened the envelope. What was inside elicited a deep gasp quickly followed by an emotional squeal of delight, not unlike a little animal. Contained inside the envelope was a wonderfully candid photograph of a young Mother with her head tossed back in laughter while cradling a very serious looking baby Vime against her bosom. It was a portrait which radiated pure joyous bliss in abandon. Vime's eyes shone as she remained captivated with the precious tender moment, forever captured and contained in that simple black-and-white photograph. This was the Mother she loved and remembered.

'Oh, Apfuo! Where did you find this'? Vime flung herself into Father's arms, her heart bursting with emotion. Photographs were rare and Vime did not have any picture of her and Mother together.

'A friend had tested his brand-new camera on your mother and you many years ago but never got around to get the photos printed. I asked him for the negatives which he had fortunately preserved and got it printed yesterday. I thought you'd like to have it. I have one for Neime too.'

Father and daughter fondly reminisced for some time as they often did these days. Remember the time we spent Christmas and New Year in the village and how Mother insisted everyone stay up all night on New Year's Eve? How Mother loved waking Vime and Neime at first dawn on birthday mornings with kisses and a gift. Remember those impromptu picnics in the fields that Mother always initiated? Remember, remember? someone would ask needlessly; yes, yes of course, how I can forget, came the faithful reply, always.

In the years to come, an older Vime and Neime would reflect how it was rather bittersweet that their father should become a better, more present Father only after Mother's passing. But such are the ironies of life.

After Father left, Vime lovingly and tenderly stroked Mother's face on the starkly monochromatic photograph, her heart full, eyes brimming with unshed tears, happy and sad both.

She heard Khrielie call down below, 'Vime, please come down and help with dinner!'

Vime got up and carefully propped the portrait against the wall on the little wooden study table beside her bed. She made a mental note to purchase a frame tomorrow, or perhaps she would try and make one herself. Just as she was closing the door to leave, the last light of day gloriously streamed through the open window, flooding the room with its soft golden glow, washing Mother and little Vime in all hues of colour imaginable. Vime felt her breath catch. She held a wondrous steady gaze upon the picture, transfixed, as their images danced under heaven's light. Finally, Vime closed the door with a soft gentle click.

ACKNOWLEDGEMENTS

My heartfelt gratitude goes to Rea Mukherjee—for her immense faith and invaluable inputs in this book's journey. My sincere thanks to Aparna Abhijit, for editing the manuscript with such care and patience.

I remain forever indebted to storytellers and oral narrators who have generously shared their knowledge with me, and taught me how to listen.

Finally, to my amazing parents and family, as ever, for their unwavering love and encouragement. I am truly blessed.